Memories
of the
Soul

Dear Sheila,

Beautiful, laugh-filled memories are the most cherished gifts we can give the people we love.

Wishing you the Best,
Barbara Yates

Dear Sheila,

Beautiful, laugh-filled memories are the most cherished gifts we can give the people we love.

Wishing you the Best,
Barbara Jahn

Memories of the Soul

Barbara Yates

Copyright © 2013 by Barbara Yates.

Library of Congress Control Number: 2013907007
ISBN: Hardcover   978-1-4836-2675-8
               Softcover   978-1-4836-2674-1
               Ebook   978-1-4836-2676-5

All rights reserved. No part of this book may be reproduced or transmitted in any form or by any means, electronic or mechanical, including photocopying, recording, or by any information storage and retrieval system, without permission in writing from the copyright owner.

This is a work of fiction. Names, characters, places and incidents either are the product of the author's imagination or are used fictitiously, and any resemblance to any actual persons, living or dead, events, or locales is entirely coincidental.

This book was printed in the United States of America.

Rev. date: 05/07/2013

To order additional copies of this book, contact:
Xlibris Corporation
1-888-795-4274
www.Xlibris.com
Orders@Xlibris.com
133739

I dedicate this book to my Mother, in Heaven.

You told me 30 years ago that I could write one, it just took me a long time to believe you. I guess I should have listened sooner.

I miss you.

Prologue
May 31, 2013

Sitting up in bed, after yet another sleepless night of turmoil, I realized I can't continue with this madness my life had become. Since waking from a coma a month ago, screaming at the top of my lungs with the agony I was feeling and scaring the hell out of my sister, Bronwyn, I've tried to get my family to listen, to understand, to believe.

None of them could even begin to imagine the sheer terror, and heartache I had gone through to come back to them, the sound of Jacob's grief-stricken voice crying out my name, etched in my mind forever.

They tried to calm my anguished ramblings with talk of nightmarish, and coma induced dreams. It wasn't a damn dream! Dreams were short events that started and ended quickly, not a long narrative that lasted for hours, and days, and months.

My family, thinking I'm in a state of depression, have forced me to see every type of doctor imaginable, mostly specialist of a psychological nature. I remember at one of these visits reading my name on my chart, *Jacobs, Caitlyn*, the irony causing a rush of uncontrollable tears.

I wanted to shriek at them, "I'm not depressed damn it, I'm in mourning."

The man I love to my very core is gone, most likely dead, and the not knowing was driving me crazy, the loss, torture to my soul. It had happened, all of it, and no one believed me. I finally gave up trying to make them.

The last six months of my life with Jacob had brought me the happiest of joys, exquisite pleasure, gripping fear, and now the worst, extreme sorrow, and I was determined to find some proof that it had all truly happened. No amount of doctors, with their fancy degrees, were going to convince me otherwise.

With renewed determination I got out of bed and went to my desk, switching on my computer and wondering why I hadn't thought of this sooner.

Sitting down, I typed in my favorite genealogical website. When it came up I went to the search window and started typing: Jacob Samuel Wilkinson, New York, USA, date of birth, November 30, 1852.

The Beginning

"Sometimes the Soul must make a journey to find it's mate, and become whole"

Jacob
November 7, 1882

Living in the North Country of New York all my life I have become somewhat adept at predicting the onset of an early Autumn storm and from the appearance of the darkening sky, and the crispness of the blustery air, I sensed one was soon to be upon us.

Preparations for an oncoming storm are numerous on a farm and I'm glad I got an early start. Chopping wood for the fireplaces and stoves took up a good portion of my morning followed by inspections to the cabin's shutters and doors. I made a thorough sweep of the barn, cleaning out the horse stalls, making ready the cow pen for my two milk cows, and laying fresh hay for all. I had an inside coop that the chickens instinctively moved to when they sensed a storm and I already noted the arrival of the bad tempered rooster in the rafters.

Everything seemed to be in proper order, no loose nails, screws, or latches to fix, making the task of securing my home fairly effortless from here. Another reason I kept myself busy was Caitlyn, my mind obsessed by her. She hadn't made her usual Autumn visit as of yet, and I was afraid if she didn't get here soon it would be too late.

With my chores complete I decided to get cleaned up knowing that once the temperature dropped it would be too damn cold to consider getting wet. As I stepped out of the tub, a strong sense of awareness hit me. She's here! Quickly dressing I bounded down the stairs and out the door, calling over my shoulder to my two dogs who apparently wanted to follow, to stay.

My pace quickens as I walk the path leading to the waterfall, knowing the pleasure I'll feel when I finally lay my eyes on her again. For 22 years I've watched her growing from a laughing child into the beautiful woman she has become. Envisioning her brings a smile to my face. Her long thick hair the color of copper shining in the sun, her sparkling sapphire eyes full of life, and that body of hers, my God, it makes me hungry for a lot more than food. She is honestly the most beautiful woman I've ever seen, but unfortunately we've never actually met.

Arriving at the falls I make my way up to the entrance of the cave that's concealed behind the curtain of water, trying as always, to figure out why I'm able to depart 1882 and come out on the other side of the cave, someplace in the future. It all began a few days before my 8th birthday in the Autumn of 1861.

Getting ready for bed, my mother had kissed my forehead and wished me a good night, my best friend in the whole world, Old Bear, curled up at the foot of my bed where he always slept. He was my constant companion, drooling and slobbering on me since the day I was born according to my parents. He was slowing down a bit, getting close to 13 years old which was up there for a Newfie, but he was always willing to go where I wanted to go, which at my age, was pretty much everywhere.

We lived on a 1,000 acre farm located in the foot hills of the Adirondack mountains. There was an abundance of apple, cherry, and maple trees, vines full of hanging clusters of grapes, and strawberry and blueberry bushes that yearly were laden with fruit. My mother knew how to make good use of our nature's bounty by making the most mouth watering cookies, pies, and jams. The farm also produced squash, cabbage, corn, and snap beans which were edible I guess, but I'm not raving.

I loved the dogs! We bred Newfoundlands, the most lovable breed of dog you could come by, if you asked me. Newfies were covered with long, velvety fur and as big as bears, especially to a young boy who hadn't hit any of his major growth spurt as of yet.

One of my chores was to help with the dogs, feeding, grooming, and cleaning out pens, especially when there was a litter of pups, at least one per year. The pups were fun but they increased my work load considerably, and decreased my free time, which me and Old Bear enjoyed using to explore every inch of our 1,000 acres.

Memories of the Soul

The next morning I woke up bright and early to the smell of breakfast cooking. The pungent aroma of frying bacon was better than the mean old Rooster at getting the day started. My Ma was the best cook. Truthfully the only other person's cooking I had ever eaten was Hattie Mae's, who lived on the other side of the orchard. Thankfully when my little sister was born Hattie Mae came over to help out because my Pa had tried, giving Ma a few days to rest, but cooking was not his strong point.

I got myself dressed and headed down the stairs calling out to Old Bear to come on as I raced for the kitchen. When I reached the bottom of the steps and realized he wasn't following me I got an uneasy feeling in the pit of my stomach. When I called out again and he didn't appear I headed back upstairs, fear slowing my step.

Bear was curled up on his old rug and seemed to be sleeping soundly, but when I bent down and rubbed my hand over his big soft head he didn't move. Intense pain shot through me, and I let out a cry that brought my parents running. When they entered the room and saw Bear on the floor they realized what had happened and tried to comfort me. Tears flooded my eyes and I turned and blindly ran down the stairs, out the door, as far and as fast as I could go.

When I finally came to a stop I was at the waterfall. It was a favorite place of mine. I loved to just sit and watch the falls, the sound of the flowing water always seemed to calm me. I saw the rocky path up the steep cliff's face and even though I knew I wasn't suppose to, I began to climb. I just wanted to hide behind the water and cry for the loss of my best friend.

In all the times I had come here I had never braved the climb, my parents had warned me not to because they felt it was too dangerous. When I reached the ledge I was surprised to find a small carved out area behind the curtain of water complete with a jutting rock that was a perfect seat.

I sat there crying, where no one could see me, just thinking about Old Bear and knowing how much I was going to miss him. When I finally cried myself out I started to notice my surrounding. It was peaceful in here, the water rushing down the side of the cliff, hiding me from the world.

All of a sudden I heard the muffled sound of laughter reminding me of my little sister's childish giggles when I tickled her. I peeked out from around the water thinking that my parents had somehow followed me, but found that I was still alone. Hearing the laughter again I realized it was coming from behind the water. I went back in past the rock seat to the other side and found a narrow, concealed opening that led into a small cave. I sure wished that Old Bear was with me now because I was really nervous about exploring the cave alone.

I heard the laughing again, louder this time, and I followed the sound seeing light coming through a gap ahead of me. When I reached the opening I peeked out and saw a short path through a wooded area that lead to two tall matching trees. I followed the path, walking between the two identical trees, and came out in a clearing, finding the source of the laughter.

She couldn't have been more than 5 years old with curly reddish blond hair and the biggest blue eyes I'd ever seen. She was chasing a butterfly, giggling every time it fluttered away just out of her reach. There was a lady with her, most likely her mother, who was holding a small baby girl in her arms. I heard the woman call out, "Caitlyn, come back over this way honey." I stood there and watched her run after the butterflies, stopping every so often when a flower caught her eye.

After watching for a while I noticed that they were dressed in odd clothes. Caitlyn had on some kind of one-piece thingy that showed her chubby little legs as she ran and played. Even her mother's clothes were different from anything my mother had ever worn.

My curiosity forced me closer and I watched as Caitlyn turned, looked in my direction, and ran right towards me. Stopping directly in front of me, she just stood there, staring at me.

Looking back, I smiled and said, "Hello."

After a few seconds she turned and ran back towards her mother like she hadn't heard or seen me at all. I watched them for a while longer and decided to try to get their attention by waving my arms and yelling, "Hello, Hello, Hello!"

Nothing, no response from any of them. I stood and watched them until they started to leave and I yelled, "Goodbye," finally realizing that I was invisible to them.

After they left I decided I better get home, figuring my parents were probably wondering where I was. I walked back up to where I thought the cave opening was but I couldn't find it. Getting panicky I ran back and forth along the rocky face until I spotted the twin trees. Running around them and back through, I immediately found the path and the cave opening.

With my heart pounding I tore through the cave, and out the other side, quickly climbing down the rocks and running for home.

That was the first time I had seen Caitlyn. I managed to sneak back a couple of times that Spring to see her again, climbing up to the cave and going through, always using the twin trees to guide me back. I never told my parents about the hidden cave, it was my secret, and I would go visit many times over the following years.

As time went by I learned Caitlyn's routine of visiting every Spring and Autumn and I would go on my time travel visits. With the first snow storm the waterfall would freeze over blocking the entrance until the Spring thaw when the waters began to flow again.

It's now the beginning of November, 1882, I'm on the verge of my 30th birthday and for the past 22 years I've watched Caitlyn grow up from that bubbly little girl to a stunning woman.

I still attempt to get her to see me, to hear me, but it's futile. Sometimes she seems to be talking to me, or maybe it's just to herself, I'm not sure. I've even tried to touch her a couple of times but my hand just passed through her, ghost like. I feel like there must be some reason that I've been given this ability to move through time, some higher purpose to finding Caitlyn that I still haven't figured out yet. "Please God, let there be a reason."

Caitlyn
November 7, 2012

Heaven on Earth! That's the best way to describe the magnificent forested valley where my Grandparents live. Twice a year since our births my parents have brought me and my little sister here on vacations, sometimes more often when there was a special occasion of some kind. Our usual stay was for two weeks in the early Spring and early Fall and the beauty of these seasons in upstate New York are almost indescribable.

On our last visit this past Spring the forest foliage was alive with brilliant shades of green, sprinkled with blooming fragrant flowers of almost every color imaginable. The crystal clear stream that runs through the woods attracts the wildlife, giving them a "nature made" drinking fountain, and brings with it the calming sounds of trickling water. My love of photography makes this the perfect palate for my camera and I've won quite a few photo contests with the striking nature images I've been able to capture here.

This is my special place, this lushly wooded area that I call my Secret Garden. It's hard to explain the way it invites me, I just feel at home, at peace, here. These feeling began for me around the age of 5 when I first sensed someone watching me, not in an ominous or uncomfortable way, more friendly, and tender. I've never actually seen anyone, but almost every time I visit this magical place, I'm aware of a presence.

Over the years, when I'm alone, I've even conversed with my invisible friend. Chatting about the beauty surrounding me, the weather, or whatever pops into my mind. No one ever answers me of course, but I feel like he is listening. I don't know what makes me think it's a he, but "he" just feels right.

I arrived for my Fall visit later than usual this year. By waiting a couple of weeks my whole family was able to get here together and we planned our stay to include a wonderful family Thanksgiving. Grandma and Grandpa really seem to enjoy the times when the whole family can get here together.

I always come every Spring and Fall, you couldn't keep me away, but sometimes my parents can't make it, or my sister can't get time off from work, so our visits are usually staggered. It was a rare treat when all the Jacobs' could get here at the same time. My sister, Bronwyn, or Wynie as I was fond of calling her, was driving up tonight, and all of us were going to the airport tomorrow to pick up my parents.

Arriving a few days ahead of the rest of my family I spent the first couple of days visiting with my Grandparents and going over the extensive menu and recipes for all the delicious foods Grandma and I were planning to prepare for our Thanksgiving feast. Mom was an excellent cook but my Grandmother was the expert. Over the years she has taught me everything she knows about cooking, rarely using recipes, and showing me how to whip up the most delicious, mouth watering baked goods without even measuring the ingredients. Even I have to admit that my version of her Apple Crisp is "To Die For."

With the menu set, I was anxious to check out, and capture with my camera, the late Autumn scenery in my secret garden. My usual visits were in October and I was curious to see how different things looked in November. I clipped my fully charged I-pod full of my favorite songs inside my jacket pocket, slung my camera strap around my neck, and was off. Grandma called out a warning for me to watch the weather because they were expecting a storm with possible snow. I sure hoped that the rest of my family arrived before the storm hit, and being from Florida, I was really looking forward to a "white" Thanksgiving.

When I arrived at my special place I noticed that most of the autumn colored leaves had already fallen off the trees and were clustered in huge piles of vivid oranges, crimsons, and yellows around the stark brown trunks. The contrast between the bare branches and the colorful leaves created an inspiring image and I quickly pulled my camera from around my neck, looked through the view finder and started snapping away happily.

I moved from subject to subject taking a variety of shots of each scene that I found through my lens. I could hear thunder rumbling in the distance and thought about my Grandmother's warning, hoping I wouldn't have to cut my photography session short. I realized that no matter when I visited this location it was always beautiful, and totally photogenic.

I continued shooting picture after picture, all the while visualizing in my mind how fantastic it was going to be to download these images later, when all of a sudden I felt a slight chill, and goose bumps raise on my skin. Awareness washed over me as I lowered my camera thinking, "He's Here!" I glanced around, looking, and at the same time knowing, I wouldn't see anyone.

"Hello Friend," I whispered. "I was afraid I might miss you this visit because of my late arrival."

I raised my camera and started looking through the view finder waiting for my eye to fall upon my next picture as I spoke aloud to my surroundings, "I hope your well."

As I moved along to the next beautiful scene I continued my one sided conversation, "It sure is beautiful here this time of year, I've always missed this by coming in October."

Some people might think I was totally bonkers talking to myself but I really felt like "he" was listening.

The breeze seemed to be picking up as I heard another rumble of thunder. "I may have to call it a day if the weather gets any worse," I said aloud just as I became aware of the two tall thin trees standing about four feet apart directly in front of me, the darkening sky behind them. They were like a pair of skinny twins forming an entryway that I had never noticed, or photographed before.

I lifted my camera to my eye, adjusting the focus on the two trees, and there he was standing between them, arms crossed, smiling at me while leaning his shoulder against the narrow trunk of the tree on the right.

He was the most attractive man I had ever seen. Instinctively I pushed the shutter button, and at exactly the same moment, I heard the explosion, and felt myself being propelled through the air as the tree behind me shattered. The last thing I remember was hitting him square in his chest as my head hit the tree . . . then nothingness.

Jacob

As I walked towards the waterfall I couldn't help but notice the increasing chill in the air. I felt sure Winter would be setting in early this year and was glad that I had already taken care of the majority of Winter prep that needed doing. There was always work to get done when you ran a farm but there was no way I was giving up, possibly my only chance, of seeing Caitlyn. I sure hoped my intuition was correct and that she had arrived, if not I may not be able to see her again until next Spring. Over the years I have tried many various ways to get to her side, besides the cave opening, without success.

As I climbed the rocks I noticed that the spray from the falls was getting colder so I hurried to the cave and made my way through. When I came out and walked the short path to the twin trees I was pleasantly surprised to catch sight of her right away. She usually roamed about, taking pictures with her fancy little camera, but she never seemed to venture so close to this side. I paused between the two trees, leaning comfortably against one, and took in the gorgeous view, of her. My God it felt good to see her again.

Suddenly she stopped mid picture and turned, glancing around and shivering slightly. "Hello Friend." I heard her whisper. Hearing her voice was such a gift for my lonely ears. I didn't spend much time with other people, kind of a loner, besides being too busy with the farm, so a human voice, especially hers, was an undeniable treat.

She seemed to be in a chatty mood and I couldn't help smiling as I listened to her, watching as she moved closer to my resting place. She turned directly towards me and raised her camera, focusing on the trees I was standing between, her hair lifted by the increasing breeze, whipped around her head. I saw her face register sudden surprise, and heard the clicking sound of her camera, at the exact same moment the bolt of lightning hit the tree behind her and exploded.

Caitlyn's body was hurled through the air with such force, hitting me in the chest and knocking me backwards onto the path with her landing on top of me. Besides her terrified scream I also heard the crack of her head as it hit the tree I was leaning against. When I sat up with her in my arms I could already see a nasty welt forming above her left temple. She was out cold. I immediately checked for her pulse, surprised by the feel of her warm neck, and was blessedly relieved when I found one. She was alive!

As I stood up with her in my arms the skies opened up and torrents of frigid rain soaked us to the skin. Pausing for a brief moment, not knowing what to do, I looked back at the trees and saw her body laying on the ground. Shocked, I looked back down at her in my arms and wondered how it was possible that I could be holding her and seeing her laying there at the same time?

I didn't have much time to wonder as another bolt of lightning struck close by stirring me into action. I turned in the direction of the cave and ran, carrying Caitlyn's limp body as I rushed through and out the other side. The water from the fall had turned icy and I had to be careful climbing down the slippery rocks while shielding her in my arms, but I managed it as quickly as possible and headed for my home.

Coming out of the woods and approaching the cabin I could see my dogs through the beginning snow flurries, alert on the porch, obediently awaiting my return where I had told them to stay. When I got to the steps I could tell that Bear and Griz were curious about who I was carrying in my arms, but they didn't make a move, waiting for my commands as to what they should do. "Good Boys," I said, as I navigate around them heading for the door.

I got Caitlyn inside and laid her on the couch where I quickly removed all of her wet clothes, pausing momentarily to take pleasure in the sight of her body, and then wrapping her in a warm quilt. I went to the fireplace and added a couple of logs to build up the fire and get the chill out of the cabin. The storm outside was intensifying and it looked like we were in for an early Nor'easter.

I ran up to the bedroom, stripping off my sodden clothes as I went, replacing them with dry. I stoked the wood stove with plans of moving Caitlyn up here as soon as the room was warm, all the while having my trailing dog's rapt attention. They seemed to be totally engrossed in what I was doing, patiently waiting in case I had some important task needed from them.

"Go watch her," I commanded as I search for something warm I could put on Caitlyn. They dutifully headed down the stairs to take up watch of my injured visitor.

Grabbing one of my flannel shirts I bounded down the stairs stumbling once but managing to catch myself before crashing head first to the floor below. I wouldn't be much help to Caitlyn if I was unconscious, or dead. I rushed to her and opened the blanket, pulling her up against me I slid her arms into the warm shirt as I inspected her to see if she had any other injuries that needed tending. Finding none, I laid her back down, buttoned her up and then rewrapped her in the quilt.

The welt above her temple was swollen and turning a deep shade of purple. I rushed to the door and looked outside, thankful that the snow was falling heavy and already forming a drift close to the porch. I ran out and grabbed a handful and packed it into a rounded out ball and wrapped it in a small towel. Returning to her I placed the ice gently on the bump and held it there in an attempt to bring down the swelling, repeating the process and making fresh snow balls as the ones before melted.

After about an hour the swelling stopped, and even seemed to have gone down slightly. During this whole process Caitlyn hadn't stirred. Her pulse and breathing were strong and steady but she was still unconscious. I carefully lifted her and carried her to the bedroom upstairs and placed her on the bed, removing the quilt that had gotten damp from the ice and covering her with the dry one from the bed. She looked like she was sleeping peacefully and I stood there looking at her, amazed at how good she looked in my bed. Now if I could only see those beautiful blue eyes of hers.

For the next two days I watched over Caitlyn like a hawk never leaving her side for more time than was absolutely necessary. Every few hours I would turn her, changing her position, then tuck her back in so she'd stay warm. Whenever I was forced to go out to the barn to care for my animals I made sure to leave Bear guarding over her. He was a huge animal and quite intimidating, but as gentle a beast as you'd ever want to meet. I knew he'd alert me if she woke, yet I still rushed about and got back to my bedside vigil as quickly as possible. Sometimes this wasn't easy as the snow storm that had started two days earlier was still ragging with only the slightest sign of slowing down. We were definitely going to be snowed in for a while.

I sat down in the rocking chair I had pulled up next to the bed, worn out from lack of sleep and worry, and simply looked at her laying there turned on her side facing me. The swelling on her left temple had gone down considerably leaving a bruise that was still dark blue and purple in color. If she would just wake up I believed she'd be okay. How many more days could she be out? I yawned feeling exhaustion take over my body, as my eye lids closed my last thought was, "Come on Caitlyn, open those pretty eyes of yours."

Grandma & Grandpa
2012

Ruth had been watching the darkening sky since Caitlyn had taken off on her photo expedition into the wooded area of the valley, her thoughts on all her family members who were expected to arrive over the next 12 hours. Bronwyn this afternoon, and her daughter and son-in-law tomorrow morning. The weather reports weren't looking good and she was starting to fret about whether, or not, they would all be able to get here safely as planned. Bronwyn was due any time and Ruth felt sure she would beat the storm, but her daughter's flight was not scheduled until the next morning and if this approaching storm was as bad as predicted they might be forced to close the airport.

Another loud rumble of thunder returned her thoughts to Caitlyn, tromping around through the trees with lightning moving closer. She knew how dangerous it was out there when a storm was looming and Ruth hoped Caitlyn was smart enough to be on her way home.

With that thought still fresh in her mind the earsplitting crack and deafening explosion caused her to jump a foot off the ground and sent her scrambling to the family room in search of her napping husband. She intended to send him out immediately in the jeep to pick up their Granddaughter. When she got to Charlie he was sitting upright having been startled awake by the loud blast. "That one hit something," he shouted out as he rose from the chair. "Is Caitlyn back?"

"No," Ruth informed him as he got up, picked up his keys and headed out the door. "Be careful," she called after him, "Here, take the cell phone."

Charlie drove down the dirt road that he knew Caitlyn always used on her walk back to the house. He was surprised when he got to the end and he hadn't found her. Getting out of the jeep he headed down the pathway to the clearing where she had always played as a child, still not finding her.

He moved towards the opposite side of the clearing as the winds picked up and the temperature dropped sharply. Lightning was still shooting across the darkening sky as he continued his search. He spotted the huge tree that had been struck, still smoking, with large chunks of bark blown out and scattered all around the base. His eyes scanned the area, and that's when he finally found her, lying face down between two thin trees.

He ran to Caitlyn, his eyes filling with tears as he approached her still form. With fear griping at his chest he checked for her pulse and was relieved to feel the steady beat. He turned her over finding her unconscious, but alive and breathing. He saw the darkly bruised lump on her temple and knew he needed to get her to the hospital. He called 911 on his cell giving them all the information needed and then lifted his precious granddaughter, carrying her, as quickly as he was able, to the jeep.

When he returned to the house minutes later Ruth came rushing out the door, the sound of the siren getting louder as it approached. The ambulance pulled into the drive followed by their granddaughter, Bronwyn. "What happened?" she yelled as she jumped out of her car running towards her family.

"Caitlyn's been hurt," Charlie said as he put his arm around her shoulder and pulled her to him for support. Ruth hovered as the paramedics moved Caitlyn to a stretcher and began working on her.

"What happened to her?" Ruth begged her husband for answers.

"I don't know Ruthie, I found her not far from a tree that had been struck by lightning. She was unconscious when I found her."

The wind was whipping around them, chilling them as the snow flurries began whirling in the air. The EMT's loaded Caitlyn into the waiting ambulance and checked her vital signs, prepping her for the trip to the Emergency Room. Charlie told them which hospital to take her to and let them know that they'd meet them there.

They arrived at the ER and found the Doctor examining Caitlyn, writing orders for blood work, x-rays, a CAT scan, and an MRI of her head. Charlie filled the doctor in on what he knew about her injury while Bronwyn and Ruth took care of all the registration and insurance paperwork.

A member of the nursing staff started an IV and hooked Caitlyn up to a machine that periodically checked her blood pressure. During all the needle poking, staff activity, and noise going on around her, Caitlyn just laid there unmoving, and oblivious of the fear that had her family in it's grip.

Charlie left the room and went out to the waiting area so he could call his daughter and son-in-law and let them know what had happened. When he glanced out the front window he saw that the snow fall had increased considerably and that the chances of them flying in tomorrow morning were dwindling.

After talking with his daughter he returned to Caitlyn's room and waited for the doctor to bring some news. After a couple of hours, and numerous trips to different departments for testing, the doctor finally came to the waiting family with what he could tell them so far.

All of Caitlyn's vital signs were good. Her EKG and EEG had no abnormalities. The contusion on the side of her head did not cause any bleeding on her brain. They were going to admit her and move her to a hospital room where they could continue to monitor her brain activity.

"She's in a state of complete unresponsiveness, a coma," the doctor stated "Periods of impaired consciousness can be short, or long, we'll just have to take it a day at a time," he said grasping Ruth's hand for encouragement.

Bronwyn could see that her Grandparents were exhausted and told them to go on home and rest before they got snowed in here and wouldn't be able to leave. "I'll stay with her tonight and if you can get back in the morning, I'll go home for awhile and get some sleep then."

Her grandparents hesitantly agreed and told her they would call her parents and update them on Caitlyn's condition.

"She's going to be alright Grandma and Grandpa, She's strong, she'll be alright," Bronwyn told them trying to convince herself as much as them. Saying a little silent prayer, "Please God, let my sister be alright."

Caitlyn

1882

Slowly waking up, I opened my eyes and gazed around the unfamiliar room wondering where I was. It was a cozy room decorated in beautiful antiques, the over-sized bed I was in felt comfortable and warm. As I shifted my gaze to the side of the bed my eyes fell on a man, asleep in the rocking chair next to the bed. With a jolt of recognition, I thought, "It's him."

Since he appeared to be sleeping soundly I let my eyes wander, taking in his lean, well-built body, his arms, muscular and strong. He was quite tall, his legs stretched out in front of him, and crossed at the ankles.

His tousled brown hair was on the longish side and swept back away from his face giving a clear view of a few days growth of beard covering his cheeks and chin. His head was leaning back against the chair, eyes closed, and his face relaxed in sleep. "Attractive," I thought, "nice nose—real nice lips—Damn, he was more than attractive, he was hot!"

Feeling stiff and sore I tried stretching slightly and was instantly startled when a huge furry head, with big brown eyes, popped up and stared right in my face causing me to let out a slight cry.

"Down Bear," my now awake companion ordered the enormous dog, who instantly dropped back down below my line of vision.

"You don't have to be afraid, he won't hurt you," he said leaning forward in his chair and staring me in the face. His blue eyes looking directly into mine with concern.

"I'm not afraid, he just surprised me," I told him my voice scratchy from lack of use. He smiled, showing off the most charming dimples on his cheeks. The words, "devilishly handsome," came to mind.

I needed to move, stretch, sit up, my body beginning to ache in it's prone position. My throat felt so dry it was hard to swallow and the need for a drink became the upper most thought in my mind. "Do you think I could have a glass of water?" I asked hoarsely.

He sprung from his chair, quickly walking across the room to a small table containing a pitcher and glass, and poured me some. Returning to the bed he helped me sit up and handed me the glass, seeming to get great pleasure in watching me drink. I really could have guzzled down the whole damn pitcher so when he asked if I wanted more I smiled and shook my head in the affirmative.

My request also afforded me a chance to watch him walk across the room and back again, his gait agile, and manly. In all my life I had never found a man so attractive. After guzzling down the second glass of water I felt I could finally speak without croaking. "I'm Caitlyn Jacobs," I said, extending my hand to shake.

My action brought out his finest smile so far, as he reached out and took my hand in his warm two handed grasp. "Nice to meet you Caitlyn Jacobs, I'm Jacob Wilkinson."

Smiling at the fact that are names were the same, I said, "Nice to meet you too, Jacob," noticing how he didn't seem to want to let go of my hand that was swallowed up by his much larger ones.

My stomach made an odd growling sound bringing with it the thought of much needed food. Chuckling, he asked, "Are you hungry?"

"Starving to death," I answered, as my stomach made it's emptiness obvious with another loud gurgle.

Laughing he said, "If you think you can make it down to the kitchen I'm sure I can scrounge up something for you to eat."

I immediately sat up, swinging my legs over the side of the bed, at the same time realizing I was only wearing a shirt. I saw his eyes dart to my bare legs then quickly look away as if the sight of them caused him discomfort. He got up and went to a beautifully carved, Armoire and after rifling through the hanging clothes pulled out a long robe. Coming back to the bed he handed it to me saying, "This should fit."

"Thank you," I said as I slid my arms into the comfy sleeves wondering who the robe belonged to. "Lady friend's?" I asked, bringing the smile back to his face momentarily.

"No," he answered, "It had belonged to my mother. My parents passed away, a little over a year ago in an accident, and I haven't had the heart to move all of their stuff yet." I could tell from his expression that these memories were still painful.

"I'm sorry Jacob," I said, as the thought of my family came to mind and I asked, "Do my Grandparents know where I am?"

With concern creasing his brow he said, "I'm not really sure, we need to talk. Let's go downstairs and get you some food, and I'll tell you what I can."

Standing up I was hit with a wave of dizziness and had to immediately sit back down.

"Here, let me help you," he said taking my arm and helping me stand. I still felt extremely shaky, which he immediately noticed, so he bent down and picked me up in his arms saying, "I think this will be the easiest, and safest, way to get you down the stairs."

Let's just say, I wasn't complaining. Being in his strong arms gave me a comforting feeling of security.

Coming out of the room and descending the staircase I was enthralled by the beauty of the log cabin. I had always had a fondness for them and this one was exquisite. The massive open beams overhead were all natural logs. The wood on the walls, bearing knot holes that added texture, were the richest shades of amber, and highlighted by the glow from the natural light coming in the large window near the ceiling. Each step of the staircase was a split log, sanded smooth on the top while leaving the bark on the lower curved bottom.

An inviting fire burned in the massive stone fireplace that flanked the far wall of the living room area, and was shared by the kitchen, complete with antique appliances consisting of a large wood burning stove, an ice box type refrigerator and a big copper farm style sink.

I was awe struck, it was like something right out of a magazine from 100 years ago. The presence of the two large dogs curled up on the living room floor just made it more homey.

"Your home is beautiful," I spoke softly, my eyes wide trying to take it all in.

"Thank you," he said, giving me another one of his smiles as he placed me in one of the chairs that surrounded the kitchen table.

"I met Bear upstairs, who's your other friend?" I asked glancing over at the brown dog who I thought should have bore the same name.

"That's Griz. They're big, but lovable," he informed me.

Looking over at them again, noticing the good portion of floor they took up, I felt they had both been appropriately named.

Jacob

Scrounging around the kitchen, trying to decide what to offer Caitlyn to eat, my mind was racing with thoughts of what I was going to tell her. How do you begin to explain to someone the truth about what had unbelievably happened, when I didn't even know myself. She was awake, alive, here. Her beautiful warm body had been in my arms as I carried her down the stairs. Glancing over at her every few minutes to make sure I wasn't dreaming, I finally asked, "Do you like eggs?"

She looked at me, with that glorious smile again, nodding her head yes. "Love them," she answered, "Any way you make them."

Thank God for that, I thought, because no matter how I tried, my eggs always came out scrambled.

She seemed to be quite enthralled with the cabin, her eyes darting from one thing to the next as she studied my home with a look of pleasure on her face. "I need to get up and move a little . . . do you mind if I look around?" she asked, rising to her feet but holding on to the table for support.

Watching her, as she stood, to make sure she wasn't going to fall, I told her, "Make yourself at home, just be careful until you feel steady on your feet. I don't want you to hit that pretty little head of yours again."

Giving me a quick smile she stood and starting out slowly moved around the room, stopping to look at a picture of my parents on the mantle "Are these ancestors of yours Jacob?" she asked, examining the picture closely, "You look a lot like this man."

Trying to think of an answer, and knowing that she thought we were both from the same era, I finally just said, "Yes." Quickly trying to distract her from the other photos which included one of me and my sister, I called out, "Foods ready, Let's eat."

She moved across the room and joined me at the table. I set two heaping plates of scrambled eggs, and thick slices of buttered toast on the table with a jar of Grape Jam opened and ready to spread. Two steaming cups of coffee, the final touch.

I could see Caitlyn lick her lips, in anticipation of the meal, as she sat in the side chair leaving the one at the head of the table open for me. "This smells heavenly," she said as she lifted her fork and took a big bite of egg, sighing with pleasure. "The eggs are delicious," she raved, making me quite proud of my accomplishment.

After a very short time the plates were empty, except for a few crumbs from the toast. Caitlyn insisted on washing the dishes, telling me she needed to do something to burn off some of the food she'd just eaten to keep from exploding. I helped by drying. When everything was cleaned up, I refilled the mugs with coffee, and led her to the couch. Sitting side by side, it was time to get this over with.

I explained how I had found the cave as a child and gone through and seen her. Once I got started the words tumbled out, how year after year I'd gone to the clearing and watched her as she'd grown up.

"Why didn't you ever come out where I could see you?" she questioned, never expecting the answer I was about to give.

"Caitlyn, I tried to get you to see me but you couldn't because I live in the year 1882. I don't know what year your from, but I know it's in the future." Continuing I said, "I don't know how to explain any of this, but you know that picture of my 'ancestors' you saw on the mantle . . . that's my parents, it was taken two years ago, a few months before they were killed."

Glancing back over her shoulder at the picture frame Caitlyn's face turned serious as she tried to comprehend everything I was telling her. "How did I get here, in the past with you?"

I told her about the lightning strike, how she had slammed into me standing between the trees from the force of the explosion. "I was shocked by the fact that I could touch you, and scared to death because you were hurt."

Running my hand through my hair I continued, "I picked you up in my arms and saw you lying on the ground at the same time. I didn't know which way to go, then the rain started and another bolt of lightening struck the ground close by, so I just turned and ran, bringing you here."

Her next question was painful because I didn't know the answer, "Can I go back to my own time?"

Looking at the unshed tears in her eyes, I said, "I don't know what happened to the part of you I left behind . . . if your future body is still alive or not." "I'm sorry but we won't be able to find out until the waterfall thaws next Spring, then I should be able to take you back."

Her tears spilled down her cheeks as she wept, "My poor family, this was suppose to be a special Thanksgiving and now I can just imagine what they're going through."

I wanted to put my arm around her, and comfort her, but I wasn't sure she'd want me to touch her. "I'm really sorry Caitlyn, I never meant to upset you."

She looked at me, noticing my unease. "I don't blame you, Jacob, it's not your fault. You had no control over something you couldn't understand." Laying her hand on my leg in a comforting gesture she went on, "Even though I didn't have the privilege of watching you all these years, I've felt your presence. I couldn't have left you hurt, laying on the ground either."

Trying to suppress a yawn, she said softly, "Thank you for saving me."

After another big yawn she laid her head against my chest and fell asleep.

Caitlyn

I was completely exhausted after Jacob's revelation, my emotions taking a roller coaster ride. Having seen a number of movies about time travel I never imagined I'd be playing a leading role in one. The thought of the heartache my family was most likely going through was too much for me so I had curled up against his chest and escaped it all in blissful sleep.

When I woke up to the sound of the Grandfather clock bonging in the hour of six, I had no idea whether it was morning, or night. Jacob was asleep, my head resting on his warm chest, his body looking as though it hadn't moved an inch, for fear of disturbing me. He was a kind man, I had sensed it before I even met him. It was weird, but I felt like I'd known him forever.

Moving a little I got the sudden realization that I had need of a bathroom, NOW! All the coffee earlier had filled my bladder to the point of bursting. Feeling my movement, Jacob stirred awake, and I immediately made my needs known. He showed me where the small bathroom was located on the first floor, then left, giving me privacy.

When I came out I found Jacob standing in the kitchen, adding wood to the stove. "I was thinking you might be hungry again, I could make you some more eggs," he suggested, "I'm sorry but it's really the only thing I know how to cook properly."

"I can cook, do you mind if I look around?" I asked.

Jacob did a little bow, stepping back out of my way, and said, "Feel free to nose into anything you like, the kitchen's all yours."

"Since your forced to be my host until Spring, the least I can do is take over the cooking," I informed him as he took a seat at the table intent on watching me, and in case I couldn't find something. "Flour, milk, butter, cinnamon, and sugar should do it, and a couple of apples if you have any," I instructed him.

He jumped up, gathering, and showing me at the same time, where all these items were kept. Once I had everything I needed I let my hands go to work, measuring, peeling, chopping, mixing, it felt so good to be in a kitchen. "You wouldn't happen to have a little molasses would you, and maple syrup?" I called to Jacob who jumped up to do my bidding.

He seemed to be enjoying the show, sitting at the table, close enough to see, but out of my way. I set the cast-iron skillet on one of the open flames of the stove to heat up while I finished mixing the batter. As soon as the pan was ready I added a little butter, swirling it around, and poured in the pancake batter. While the bottom side was cooking I topped the pancakes with chopped apples, cinnamon, and the brown sugar I had made out of white sugar and molasses.

When I flipped them over the aroma of the cinnamon and apples filled the room. In a matter of minutes I had a platter full of Apple Cinnamon Crunch Pancakes . . . one of my favorite recipes from my Grandmother.

Jacob had set the table so all I had to do was bring out the platter and pour the coffee. Breakfast was served as the clock gonged seven.

I ate four, enjoying every bite. Jacob polished off the rest of the platter, not talking much in the process. When he was done he pushed back from the table, smiled at me, and said, "Those were the best pancakes I've ever eaten. Thank you, I'd forgotten how good real food tasted."

I told him he was quite welcome and got busy cleaning up the kitchen. Jacob fed the dogs and took them out. When they returned he asked, "Would you like me to fill the tub for you?"

The thought of soaking in a hot tub sounded wonderful, so I told him, "That would be heavenly."

Finishing up in the kitchen, I could hear Jacob upstairs running water, and moving things around. It almost sounded like he was redecorating the whole room. After about a half an hour he came down and told me my bath was ready.

"Come on and I'll show you where everything is," he said, as he stepped back and let me lead the way up the stairs.

Upon entering I could tell that he had made the bed and straightened up. He walked over to the chest of drawers, and told me pointing, "There are clean clothes that should fit you in the right three drawers, and in the Armoire. They're not real fancy just the stuff my mother wore around the house, but I think you'll be comfortable in them."

I thanked him and headed towards the bathroom, not being able to wait another minute to get into the tub. "You can help yourself to the smelly soaps and bath things in there," he added.

Thanking him again I went into the bathroom and closed the door.

Looking around at the assortment of woman's toiletries I chose a bar of lavender soap and some old-fashioned labeled hair wash, setting them by the tub I dipped my hand in to feel the temperature of the water. "Perfect," I thought.

Removing my robe and Jacob's flannel shirt I climbed in and sunk completely under the water. After a few seconds I came up and leaned my head back against the end of the tub, relaxing there for a couple of minutes letting the glorious warmth of the water soothe me.

Sitting up I decided to start by washing my hair, then I scrubbed my entire body, and was kind of grossed out by the dirty water I left when I was finished bathing. I got out, dried off, and put the robe back on, cleaning up a bit before heading into the room.

Peeking out of the bathroom, I found the room empty and the bedroom door closed. I went over to the dresser and looked into the top drawer finding some interesting looking ladies under garments. I picked out a chemise type slip, a long petticoat, and some kind of bloomer underpants that went quite a ways down the leg, after putting them on I moved to the Armoire.

I found numerous long skirts and blouses hanging in there and picked out a nice brown skirt with a wide waistband and a cream colored blouse that was made of a soft, thicker fabric for warmth. Getting dressed I found that the clothes fit pretty well except across the chest where the blouse was pulled tight. I slipped on a pair of socks to keep my feet warm because I couldn't find any shoes.

Drying my hair as much as possible, I brushed it out and pulled it into a French braid down the back. When I was all done I was happy with my clean, fresh, 1882 look. I kind of hoped Jacob would be too. I put everything away and headed for the door.

When I arrived downstairs the cabin was quite, no dogs, and no Jacob. I decided to use my time to rummage around the kitchen and pantry area to see what I could find to make for our next meal. I felt like I was on a treasure hunt as I continued to find all the staples that had been used in a 19th Century kitchen. Some of the cookware, tools, and utensils were incredibly clever. I was used to all the modern electric gadgets that I used in my own kitchen at home. The thought of home sending a wave of sadness over me.

Bringing my focus back to the task at hand, I spotted a large pot on top of the cabinet and thought about all the vegetables I had glimpsed in the root cellar. Steaming hot Vegetable Soup sounded especially appetizing with the frigid temperatures outside.

I couldn't reach the pot so I pulled over the stool that was by the wall, and climbed up. The stool wasn't quite tall enough so I had to stand on tip toes and stretch as far as possible to reach the edge of the pot. Teetering on the stool is where I was when Jacob returned.

Jacob

After getting everything ready for Caitlyn's bath and escorting her up to show her where the things she would need were located, I returned to the living room and sat, my thoughts fixated on the naked woman in the tub upstairs. I had to get out of here for awhile, cool off, or down, was more like it.

Rising quickly from the chair and calling the dogs I decided to make a trip to the barn to check on the animals while letting the dogs run off some energy. Opening the door, and feeling the cold crisp air hit me in the face, helped settle my wayward imagination.

The snow had finally stopped, leaving everything covered in a thick layer of sparkling white. The dogs were ecstatic to be outside, running, jumping and barking their way down the path, through the snow, to the barn.

As I walked along behind them, trying to clear my lecherous mind, I decided that while I was there I'd pick out a nice plump chicken and surprise Caitlyn with it. My mouth watered thinking about the delicious meal she would be able to create with her cooking skills, and a fresh hen.

After making my rounds in the barn, I entered the chicken coop and shoed away the old rooster who seem to enjoy any excuse for pecking at me. Once I had collected the fresh eggs, I selected the fattest hen and quickly took care of the worst requirements of a delicious meal. I have to say, "slaughtering a chicken sure takes your mind off sex." When I was finished with the cleaning and plucking I picked up the basket of eggs and headed back to the house, knowing that by now Caitlyn was finished bathing, and safely dressed again.

Entering the front door I was dumbfounded by my view of Caitlyn, standing on a stool, her arm stretched high above her head reaching for a pot. With her back to me I got a clear view of her rear end protruding slightly as she bent forward, the wide band of the skirt emphasizing her tiny waist. Her arm in the air revealed the outline of her rounded breast hugged tightly by the fabric of her shirt. The sight of her stopped me dead in my tracks and I just stood there staring, a chicken in one hand, and a basket full of eggs in the other.

Grasping the rim of the large pot and trying to move it she started to lose her balance, wobbling slightly. My heart leaped as I raced forward, dropping the chicken and eggs on the table as I passed and grabbed a hold of her arm to steady her. "What the hell are you trying to do woman?" I bellowed. "Do you want to kill yourself?" I finished, reaching up and bringing down the heavy pot with one hand, slamming it on the counter.

Stepping down off the stool Caitlyn turned on me, hands on her hips, with a look of fury in her eyes she yelled, "I was perfectly fine, thank you very much!"

I had never seen her angry before and was surprised at how quickly it made me feel contrite. "I'm sorry, I didn't mean to yell, you just scared the hell out of me."

"Um . . . I brought you a chicken," I stammered. My feeble attempt to get back in her good graces seemed to be working when I heard her burst out laughing.

"You brought me a chicken?" she questioned, hysterical, "Most men bring a lady flowers, or candy maybe, not chickens," Her laughter warmed me, even though I knew it was aimed at me.

"So, we're having chicken?" Caitlyn asked still giggling, her anger totally forgotten. "Any special way you like it?" she went on as she grabbed the chicken and began expertly slicing it into pieces. Watching her handle that knife made me glad she wasn't mad at me anymore.

"I'll leave that up to you," I answered, still feeling a bit guilty for having yelled. "Do you need my help with anything?" When she told me she'd be fine, I decided it would be a good time for me to make a hasty exit, and head upstairs to get cleaned up.

Returning downstairs about 45 minutes later I was assailed by the appetizing aroma of chicken frying in the pan. I walked over and leaned against the wall so I could watch her. She had a tray of biscuits just out of the oven and a pot on the back flame with ears of corn simmering gently. My mouth watered and my stomach growled simultaneously.

She already had the table set and when she started bringing out the food I was ready to chow down. She waited for me to take the first piece of chicken before selecting one for herself. Everything smelled so good and the first bite of chicken was so delicious, the coating golden brown and crispy, the meat tender and juicy . . . and her biscuits, even my own mother would have been jealous of those. I ate till I couldn't force another bite. After a year of cooking for myself, this was heaven.

Glancing up I saw her watching me, a smile on her face. "You seem to have enjoyed 'my chicken' even more that I did," she quipped, her smile widening, "I can't wait to see what gift you bring me next."

Looking into her eyes I smiled back at her, feeling blessed that she was here with me, and knowing that she had completely stolen my heart.

Caitlyn

Watching Jacob devour my cooking with obvious delight, brought me such pleasure. Truthfully the real pleasure was just watching Jacob. On more than one occasion I've caught him looking at me with an expression in his eyes that caused a throbbing sensation throughout my body, a feeling I have never experienced before. Being from the 21st century I knew all about sex and desire but was a little unsure of how a 19th century woman was suppose to act.

I wanted him to hold me and kiss me, but I was afraid to make a move that might make him think I had loose morals. I'd never slept around, actually have very little sexual experience for a 27 year old woman. My friends back home often kidding me about my lack of conquests, while bragging about theirs. I just hadn't found a man that I felt strongly enough about to want to have sex with. That is until now.

My life with Jacob was serene and filled me with contentment. As the days passed he and I got into a daily routine that seemed to make us both happy. Breakfast together in the morning, followed by chores that sometimes kept him out until noon, at which time he always returned to the cabin to enjoy lunch with me. During my alone time I figured out all the intricacies of using a wood burning stove and started baking some of my favorite deserts and pastries to share with him after our evening meals.

In the afternoons if there wasn't anything to call him away we would sit together and talk, just getting to know each other. He was curious about my life and family so I told him about my parents and sister, and my grandparents, mentioning the fact, that he had my grandmother to thank for my excellent cooking skills.

I told him of my love of photography and the contests I had won with pictures taken in the valley. While explaining different things about the future like air travel, computers, and televisions, I often found myself laughing at his reactions of disbelief. He had an easy laugh, sometimes throwing his head back showing total enjoyment at something I had said, and those dimples of his, they made me determined to keep him smiling as much as possible.

Jacob shared with me, his life growing up on the farm with his parents and sister, about breeding Newfoundlands and how much fun it had been as a child playing with the litter of puppies that were born each year. I imagined him as a laughing little boy surrounded by yapping, licking, and nipping puppies.

He told me how he had given up the dog breeding after his parent's deaths because without their help the work load had just gotten to be too much. I could tell from his expression that he missed it. Listening to him relate the stories of his boyhood were so fascinating that I never once missed the modern forms of entertainment from my other life.

One afternoon, a couple of weeks after I'd arrived, Jacob had business to take care of with Samuel Williams who lived in a small cabin on the other side of his property. Jacob told me that Samuel was an ex-slave who had moved to the area, with his family, before Jacob was born. His knowledge of farm work, from his years on a plantation down south, had made him an irreplaceable asset to Jacob's father, and now to Jacob. He promised that he'd take me over one day to meet Samuel and his family.

Being left to entertain myself, and in need of a little exercise, I decided to sweep out the mud room. Looking around the room I noticed a large wash basin in the corner that appeared to be there for laundry purposes. It looked like once you filled the metal tub with water you could heat it by starting a fire in the pit below. I had no idea how to do this without possibly burning down the whole cabin, so I figured I'd ask Jacob to instruct me in the proper usage before attempting it. I found a barrel filled with dirty clothes and decided I could at least separate them, and get them ready to wash.

The first item I picked up from the hamper was a pair of Jacob's jeans. I was fascinated by the old fashioned looking Levis Strauss label on the back pocket, thinking people in the 21st century would pay big bucks for these. Next was a pair of long underwear. Holding them up I couldn't help but think how much men's undergarments had changed in 130 years, and imagined how sexy Jacob would look in a pair of Beckham briefs, better than David himself.

Returning to my sorting, I pulled out 2 more pairs of jeans and excitedly caught sight of my favorite red thermal shirt. Under the shirt was my brand new black Victoria Secret's bra that I had bought for my trip, followed by my jeans, Levi's also, but a much more modern style than Jacobs.

When I picked up my jeans the matching panties, to my bra, fell out of the leg. It was so nice to see my own clothes again. I put my bra and panties to the side, planning to take them upstairs and wash them with the lavender soap I used for my bath.

My jacket was next, and as I lifted it up getting ready to add it to the dark pile, I noticed a bulge in the top pocket, my I-pod . . . the ear buds still attached to it by the cord. I turned it over and pressed the power button and was totally amazed when it came on, showing a full charge. Sticking the ear buds in my ears, I pressed play, and the sweet sound of Lady Antebellum singing, "Just a Kiss," filled my ears.

I couldn't wait to show this to Jacob. I hadn't heard any kind of music since I'd been here and didn't know what kind, or even how, music was enjoyed in this era. It was going to be so much fun sharing this little bit of 2012 with him.

Finishing up the sorting, I grabbed my I-pod, sliding it into my skirt pocket, and headed to the kitchen to get dinner started. I couldn't wait for tonight to share my discovery with him.

Jacob

Arriving home, after a very productive meeting with Samuel, I walked in the door and found Caitlyn in what appeared to be her favorite place, the kitchen, cooking dinner while humming a melody that was unfamiliar to me. Every so often she would sing a few words revealing her soft voice which was quite pleasant to the ear. She seemed extra cheerful this evening, happy. I loved seeing her like this.

She was so caught up in her joyfulness that she hadn't heard me come in, giving me the opportunity to just take her in. God, she was beautiful. She had her hair pulled back in the braid that she was fond of wearing, little wisps of hair coming loose and framing her face. An intent look on her face as she chopped away at one of the ingredients she would be using in tonight's meal. Whatever she was making smelled delicious. I could see a loaf of steaming bread sitting on the counter fresh out of the oven. A beautiful woman who loved to cook, who could ask for more than that?

I made a noise to alert her to my presence and she gave a little start, "Oh! I didn't know you were there Jacob, you startled me," she said looking in my eyes, smiling.

I felt the tightening in my body again, and tried hard not to look like I wanted to jump over the table and attack her where she stood. Lord it took everything in me not to carry her upstairs and throw her in my bed. I wanted her . . . wanted her bad.

"How was your afternoon?" I asked trying to get my fantasies under control. She started telling me something about the mud room and laundry, but all I could do was stare at her mouth, wondering what her lips tasted like. My mind was gone, I didn't seem to have any power over it any more. When she announced that dinner would be ready in 10 minutes, it gave me the excuse to leave the room and go upstairs to wash up. She would be safe from my attack for at least another 10 minutes.

Coming down the stairs I could see the food on the table and my hunger was enough of a distraction to get my passion in check. Baked ham, mashed sweet potatoes, fresh green beans with onions, and the loaf of warm bread with butter was followed by delicious tart cherry turnovers drizzled with a sugary glaze. The woman definitely knew how to cook.

After dinner the dogs seemed to be hovering around the table so I fed them and took them out, giving Caitlin a chance to finish in the kitchen without them being underfoot.

When I came back in she was taking off her apron. I went to the fireplace, added a log to get the fire blazing, and sat on the couch waiting for her to join me. She came over and sat close enough that I could smell the soft fragrance of lavender on her. It was heavenly and painful at the same time.

She turned to me and said, "I have a surprise for you," as she pulled out a small square object from her pocket, "It's my I-pod, I found it today in my jacket."

"What's an I-pod?" I asked studying it's shinny surface which was about the size of my watch.

"Let me show you, it's easier than explaining," she held out one of the little ball ends and told me to put it in my ear. I did as she asked, and watched as she put the other end in hers. She fiddled around with the face and it lit up under her finger. "This is one of my favorite things from my time, are you ready?"

I nodded, yes, so she pushed on it again and music suddenly filled my ear. The song that started playing had a wonderful melody and as I listened to the words, about the world losing two lonely people with the odds against them, made me believe that the singer was talking about us.

As the song continued, I showed my enjoyment of her surprise, by standing and extending my hand in an offer to dance. Caitlyn stood, coming into my arms with a willingness and warmth that caused my breath to catch, and we began to sway to the beat of the music.

Holding her like this, my chin resting on the top of her head, gave me such strong feelings of love and protectiveness, that it rocked me to my core. When the first song ended, I was reluctantly about to release her when the next song started. Gathering her close again I let the music take over, and continued our lover's dance.

With the final words of the song playing in our ears, *Just a kiss Goodnight,* I lowered my head and she met me half way as I took her lips with mine. Feeling her tongue, and hearing her soft moan as she leaned into me, drove me beyond reason and I devoured her mouth with all the longing for her that I'd been holding inside for years.

"I feel like I've been waiting for you all my life Caitlyn," I told her as I slid my hands down the sides of her body, letting my finger tips play softly along the edges of her breasts that she pressed into my chest.

Reaching her hips, and moving my hands to cup her bottom, I pulled her up against me to let her feel what she was doing to me, and heard her sharp intake of breath. My own groans coming from deep within me, uncontrolled.

She looked into my eyes as she unbuttoned my shirt, and I felt her cool hands glide up and across my chest, to my shoulders. She leaned in and kissed my chest, her hands moving down my arms as she pushed my shirt off, and out of the way.

My body was on fire as I continued my assault on her mouth. When I felt hers trembling and heard her breathless plead, "Make love to me Jacob, please," it was all the incentive I needed to lift her in my arms and carry her upstairs to my bed.

Sitting next to her I slowly removed her clothes, marveling at each part of her body exposed, and now emblazoned in my mind. With Caitlin's eyes on me, I stood up for just a minute to rid myself of the last of my clothes, then laid down next to her pulling her onto my chest, and into my arms.

As soon as I felt her body on mine I knew this move had been a mistake on my part, the need in my body so intense I thought I would totally lose control, so I rolled her over and covered her. This position didn't ease my desire any better, and when I felt Caitlyn spread her legs I entered her in one deep thrust, causing her to gasp out my name.

Trying to slow down for her I held perfectly still, my breathing heavy, until I felt her lift up to envelop me deeper. Holding back now was out of the question and we quickly found a rhythm, moving together with sensual abandon, as we reached for release.

When I felt Caitlyn surrender, her spasms grasping at me, I joined her in the most blissful experience of my life.

Not having an ounce of strength left I collapsed on top of her, laying there for a minute trying to just breathe. It finally dawned on me that if I couldn't breathe, then Caitlyn was probably suffocating under the weight of my body, and with my last bit of energy I turned over pulling her back on top of me. She laid there limp, sprawled across my body, her heart pounding as hard as mine.

It took a good ten minutes before either of us could move. Caitlyn lifted her head, looking at me with her beautiful eyes, and said, "So that's what sex is like, now I understand the big draw."

But it was her next question that surprised, and delighted me. She sat up, straddling me, her face still flushed, and glowing, and asked, "Can we do that again?"

Grabbing her, I rolled her back under me and showed her, that yes, we could do it again, and again, and again.

Caitlyn

The week before Thanksgiving was pure bliss. Our lovemaking taking up a good portion of every day, and night. Jacob's touch had awakened a need in me that I would never have dreamed possible. He seemed to enjoy my sexual pursuit of him, and all it took was a certain look, and he was willing to satisfy my heart's desire.

When we weren't breaking in every area of the cabin, we talked about the upcoming holiday. Jacob informed me that this was the first official Thanksgiving. The current, 21st President of the United States, Chester A. Arthur, had passed Proclamation 254 on October 25, 1882, making November 30th the annual observance of public thanksgiving, and I was going to be here to share it with him.

I found out that it was also Jacob's birthday on the 30th, and set my mind on the task of coming up with something to give him for his special day. I didn't have the luxury of running to the mall for a gift, so I was going to have to be creative. I was planning on putting a lot of thought into it to see what I could come up with.

I planned the menu for Thanksgiving, thinking that a plump hen would be more practical for just the two of us. I made lists of things I needed for the meal, and timetables for my baking plans. If nothing else, I was very organized.

Being from Florida, I found the weather to be quite cold, and was happy to be spending so much time in the warm kitchen, enjoying one of my favorite pastimes, baking. According to Jacob, in this part of the country, temperatures around freezing were considered warm at this time of year.

Sharing my holiday traditions, and memories with him, I noticed a look of sadness in his eyes, knowing he was wondering about future Thanksgivings, and whether or not, we'd be together to create our own traditions. I'd only been here for about a month now, and even I was wondering how I was going to leave him when Spring came. I decided it was best to not think about that right now, and just enjoy our time together.

After dinner on Thanksgiving Eve, Jacob and I got cozy on the couch and spent some time listening to my, ever fully charged, I-pod. Every time I turned it on I was totally amazed to find the power full, and telling Jacob, he laughed, saying, "You traveled back in time 130 years and you can't believe your battery hasn't gone dead."

I guess when you thought about it that way it did seem trivial.

A sudden idea for Jacob's birthday present popped into my mind, and brought a sly smile to my face, which I hid from him. The more I thought about it the more I liked the idea, and I was now looking forward to seeing his reaction to my gift, tomorrow.

We shared a couple of slow dances, wrapped in each other's arms, and then headed up to bed early, the Grandfather clock bonging in 8:00 p.m. I had a busy day tomorrow, and was hoping to actually get to sleep, by at least midnight.

Jacob

Waking up to the feel of Caitlyn's hand moving across my chest, and down my rib cage, set fire to my blood. By the time her explorations moved lower my whole body was fully awake, and at attention.

Finally, blessedly touching me, her eyes snapped to my face, now aware that I was no longer sleeping. With her sexy, seductive smile she wished me a good morning, a happy birthday, and a Happy Thanksgiving. If her light kisses on my belly were any indication, I was sure I'd be having all three.

Succumbing to her sweet torture for as long as I could stand, I reached down and pulled her up the full length of my body, luxuriating in the feel of her. After a passionate kiss that left us both panting, she sat up, straddling my hips, and whispered, "Tell me what you want Jacob."

I was gone and begged, "You've got to let me in Caitlyn."

She lifted her body and gave me what I was begging for. When she finished her ride, and collapsed on my chest, I felt like I'd died and gone to heaven. It was definitely going to be a good day.

Laying like this until our breathing returned to an almost normal rate, Caitlyn leaned up, taking my face in both her hands, and kissed me with a tenderness that confirmed her feelings more than words could ever say. Then she rolled off me, jumped out of bed and announced, "I have a lot of work to do," heading to the bathroom.

When she came out, gloriously naked, I tried to convince her to get back in bed with me, to no avail. I laid there watching her as she hurriedly dress, then coming over, she gave me another quick kiss and said, "I'll meet your lazy ass in the kitchen when you finally decide to get out of that bed." Avoiding my grasp, she giggled as she headed cheerfully out the door.

By the time I got downstairs Caitlyn had breakfast ready and was already preparing something we would be enjoying later in the day for our first Thanksgiving together. The dogs were both sitting at attention, just outside the kitchen area, probably having already received a treat of the bacon she had cooked up. They adored her, she was spoiling them rotten, and I loved it.

After a hearty breakfast, which Caitlyn informed me would be the last food I would be getting until dinner was ready at 3:00 p.m., I gave her a lingering kiss and headed out to visit with Samuel and Hattie Mae. They didn't know about Caitlyn yet, and I knew if I didn't make an appearance on my birthday Hattie Mae would hunt me down.

Samuel greeted me at the door when I arrived saying, "You're here early boy, Hattie wasn't expectin ya till closer to dinner time."

"I'm afraid I'm not going to be able to make it for my birthday dinner this year, Samuel,"

"Well you better go on in and tell her that yourself. I'm gonna head on over to the barn, and stay there till she cools down from your news," Samuel said, hurrying to get as far away as possible, chuckling as he scurried along.

Shaking my head with a smile, I entered the cabin calling out a greeting. Hearing me, Hattie Mae came rushing out of the kitchen wrapping me in her motherly embrace. "Happy Birthday my boy, your early, I don't think I have enough food in this house if you start eatin now."

Hugging her back, I figured I'd better get this over with as soon as possible. "Hattie, I'm not going to be able to make it for dinner today."

Stepping back, she looked at me with a stern look on her face, asking, "What's so important that it's gonna keep you away from my Sweet Potato Pie?"

Lying to Hattie was impossible, so I decided to tell her most of the truth, leaving out just a few of the details. "I've got a visitor staying with me for the Winter," I informed her.

"Well you just bring him along with you Jacob. Any friend of yours is welcome in my home."

"Caitlyn is a she, Hattie," I stated, waiting for her reaction.

With a look of surprise, Hattie took hold of my arm and led me to the table, telling me to sit. Taking the seat across from me, she looked me in the eyes, and ordered, "Go ahead, start talkin."

I explained to her that when I met Caitlyn in the beginning of November, she was in trouble and needed my help. That she couldn't go home until Spring, so I brought her to the cabin so she'd be safe. I knew that Hattie could associate with this scenario because it echoed her own past, and saw proof of it when her eyes filled with tears from her memories.

"And what's gonna keep her safe from you Jacob?" she asked.

"I love her Hattie, I think I have since the minute I laid eyes on her," I told her. "I think about her all the time, she's in my blood. I believe she loves me too, and I'm hoping I can convince her to stay."

Hattie's face broke into a wide grin, standing up, she ordered, "You go on Jacob, get back to Miss Caitlyn. Take good care of her, and as soon as you can, you bring her around for us to meet."

Giving Hattie another hug, I told her not to worry, that taking care of Caitlyn was my top priority, and that I'd bring her over in a couple of weeks to meet the family.

Before I reached the door Hattie was at my side, her famous Sweet Potato Pie in her hand, giving it to me she said, "You take this on home with you, and you be nice, you share it with Miss Caitlyn."

Thanking her, I did what she said and headed for home, the thought of Caitlyn waiting for me hurrying me along. Looking back over my shoulder, I saw Samuel join Hattie on the porch, and I waved my farewell.

"Happy Birthday Jacob," they called out, waving back.

My visit had gone well, and the ride home was pleasant, the weather beautiful. When I got to the barn I quickly took care of the horses, fed the other animals so they'd be done for the day, and headed down the path towards the cabin, with my pie in hand.

The cabin looked beautiful, nestled in the trees, smoke rising out of the chimney. The best part of coming home was knowing Caitlyn was inside waiting for me. About halfway up the path I saw Caitlyn waving at me through the kitchen window, and was soon greeted by my dogs, who seemed more interested in what was in my hand, than me.

Walking in the door I was overwhelmed by the aroma of freshly baked cookies. Giving Caitlin a kiss, and handing her the pie, I snatched one off the platter and sunk my teeth in. Chunks of warm chocolate melted in my mouth. With a big glass of milk I could have polished off the whole platter. I grabbed another one, trying for a third, but she slapped my hand away, warning, "Don't eat too much or you won't want dinner." She really needn't worry, I was starving.

Sitting at the table so I could talk to her while she was working, I first asked if I could do anything to help her. When she told me that she had everything under control, I told her about my visit to Hattie and Samuel, explaining what I had told Hattie, and how excited she was to meet her. Caitlyn told me the feeling was mutual, and picking up the pie, she smelled it with a look of pleasure on her face, intending to get Hattie's recipe.

The next couple of hours passed in a companionable fashion. I found Caitlyn to be the most entertaining person I'd ever spent time with, at one minute talking seriously about a subject that she felt passionate about, and the next she'd have me roaring with laughter with her keen sense of humor. Looking at her I realized I wouldn't change a thing about her. She was perfect, perfect for me. When she caught me staring I was rewarded with one of her beautiful smiles.

Announcing dinner was ready, I helped her set the table. She brought out an array of side dishes centered around an Oven Roasted Chicken stuffed to overflowing with Cornbread Dressing. My mouth was watering, and when I glanced at my dogs, intently watching, you could see drool puddled on the floor in front of them. I guess we all loved Caitlyn's cooking.

After dinner, when everything was cleaned up and put away, Caitlyn announced that she was going upstairs, and didn't want to be disturbed. She gave me a quick kiss and assured me that everything was fine, and that she'd be back down shortly. I thought I saw a wicked little twinkle in her eyes, and couldn't wait to find out what was going on in that pretty little head of hers.

Caitlyn

When I originally thought up this surprise for Jacob it had sounded like an exciting idea, now that it was time to actually carry it out, I felt a bit of trepidation. Women in 2012 were a lot more open, and free, about their sexuality than they are in 1882, and I didn't want to do anything that might make Jacob feel negatively towards me. My mind went back to this morning, and the positive reception I got for my bold behavior then, so I decided to go for it.

Changing into my black Victoria Secret bra and matching thong panties, I looked in the mirror to see the effect. Feeling a warm sensation flow through me, I turned away and completed my ensemble with the black lace, buttoned up, high heeled boots that had belonged to his mother. I brushed out my hair and pulled it into a loose French braid that hung down the side and over my breast, tying it with a red ribbon. I could have danced on any pole back home, and gotten good tips, too.

Wrapping myself in my long rode, and tying it securely, I popped one of the mints in my mouth from the tin Jacob kept on the nightstand, grabbed my I-pod and headed for the door. Walking down the stairs, the sound of the heels clicking on the steps, a new wave of nervousness washed over me. When I reached the bottom I found Jacob standing by the fireplace watching me with a gentle burning stare. Giving him my most seductive smile, I murmured, "Come to me, Jacob."

He shot across the room in record time, wrapping me in his arms. Being afraid he'd see what I was wearing before I was ready, I put my hand on his chest and gentle pushed him back, saying, "I have a birthday surprise for you, but you have to do exactly what I say, Alright?"

Nodding his head, I watched his face, as his smile widened, showing off his dimples.

"It seems to be something that men in 2012 really like. I've never done it before, but I thought I'd try it out on you," I told him, as I walked towards the dining room table and pulled out one of the chairs. "I need you to sit here, keep your hands down, and promise me, no touching," I said as I gently pushed him into the chair. I saw his gulp as he promised.

Standing between his opened legs, I handed him one of the ear buds from my I-pod, which he put in his ear. Putting the other one in my ear, I slid my hand inside my robe and clipped the little square to my bra. "Are you ready?" I asked, again getting a nod of acquiescence.

With the first beats of *Not Myself Tonight by Christina Aguilera* I whipped open the front of the robe, exposing my provocative lingerie that was underneath, and started my dance using all the moves I had learned in years of Jazzercise classes, and the two Belly Dancing Classes I had laughed through with my sister. My hip flips and breast shaking getting rave reviews from our instructor.

When the second verse started I slid the robe off my shoulders and kicked it out of my way with the toe of my boot. Turning sideways I began zig-zagging my hips from side to side, keeping the beat with my body. Jacob's visible reaction giving me the confidence I needed to abandon all inhibitions, and just let the music move through me. Because of the ear buds I had to stay close, and Jacob's sitting position presented him with a bird's eye view of my bouncing breasts. More than once I had to bat his hands away, when he seemed to have forgotten the rules of my lap dance.

My dancing, and the heat growing inside of me, caused a light sheen of perspiration on my skin, making it glow. As the song ended my last move left me straddling Jacobs lap, each of my bare cheeks in his upturned hands. Looking him in the eyes, breathing hard with my exertion, I asked, "Did you like my present?"

Standing up so abruptly that he knocked over his chair, he lifting me in his hands, and I locked my legs around his waist as our lips connected. We were like two wild animals trying to devour each other as he carried me to the edge of the table. Tearing his pants open, Jacob growled into my mouth, "Do you know what you do to me Caitlyn?"

I couldn't even answer him, I was already going over the edge as he invaded me. It didn't take long before I was screaming with release, him joining me as we both reached new heights of unimaginable pleasure. Afterwards the two of us were sprawled together on the hard table sucking air, trying desperately to just breathe.

When we were finally able to move, we looked up, and found Bear and Griz sitting next to the table staring at us. The humor of it struck us both at the same time and we burst into hysterical laughter. The dogs deciding we weren't in distress, finally walked into the living room and laid down to sleep.

"You never answered my question Jacob, Did you like the lap dance?" I asked coyly.

"You can do that for me again any time you want Love, just make sure I'm your only customer."

"I love you Jacob, Happy Birthday," I told him.

"My heart belongs to you for the rest of my life Caitlyn," he said as he lifted me in his arms and carried me upstairs.

Jacob

It was a gorgeous December morning, but after the previous night with Caitlyn in my arms there could have been a monsoon outside and I would have found it gorgeous. If the past week was any indication, then I was sure Caitlyn had made a full recovery from her head injury. At the moment she was bustling about, cleaning parts of the cabin that had missed a woman's touch for too long.

I had some work to do down in the barn and decided to invite her along to get her out of the cabin for awhile. She was thrilled with the idea and asked if I could wait so she could run up and change her clothes first. I offered my help with this task, but she just smiled as she ran up the stairs calling out, "I'll be ready in just a minute."

When I heard the door opening upstairs, I looked up with plans to enjoy the show of her body as she came down the stairs. I was surprised to see her in her own clothes. Her jeans, close-fitting, showed off her lower curves to perfection, and the red shirt, hugging her waist and breasts, was unbuttoned at the top giving me a excellent view of her ample cleavage. All thoughts of the barn evaporated until I heard her say, "I'm ready."

She headed towards the door with me trailing her and slipped on her jacket, totally unaware that she had come extremely close to being ravaged. Going out behind her I held the door for the dogs, who pretty much insisted on going along.

It only took a few minutes to walk the hundred yards to the barn, the ground covered in only a couple of inches of snow made the journey trouble-free. There were times when this trip was treacherous, especially in the middle of a severe storm, but today it was refreshing.

When we reached the barn, we entered, and Caitlyn's attention immediately turned to the horses, heading directly for them. The chestnut mare, my mother's favorite, came right over to the gate, seemingly happy with the female visitor. I could hear Caitlyn murmuring softly to the horse as she petted her, then turning to me she said, "She's beautiful, what's her name?"

"My mother called her Starlight," I answered

Trying the name I heard her say, "Starlight, what a beautiful name," then turning to me she asked, "Can I ride her?"

"Of course, just be careful," I told her, finishing with, "She's gentle, but a little spirited. My mother loved her."

Caitlyn grabbed the bridle hanging next to the stall and did a little bend-step through the gate. I could tell she'd done this before. I watched as she slid the bridle on the mare's head, grabbed the reins, and led her out of the stall. Instructing Caitlyn I said, "Hold her and I'll saddle her for you."

"That won't be necessary," she answered, smiling, I watched as Caitlyn pulled the reins over the horses head and grabbed a handful of Starlight's mane, bending her left leg up behind her from the knee, she said, "Just give me a leg up."

Grabbing her bended leg, I hoisted her up as she swung her other leg over and mounted the horse bareback. Starlight pranced around a little, not having been ridden in quite a while. I stayed close, a little worried as Caitlyn tried to get her under control, then watched as Caitlyn grasped the reins in her left hand and tightened her legs against the horses flanks.

Starlight calmed, sensing Caitlyn's skill as she led her around the barn and towards the door. When they reached the opening I saw Caitlyn give a light kick with her heels, and at the same time let out a clear, "Yaa!" Starlight took off like a bullet.

I quickly grabbed the other bridle and threw it on Champ, swinging myself up on the stallion's back. Champ seemed as anxious to catch up to his lady as I was to catch up to mine. When I came out of the barn I saw Caitlyn, flying at a full gallop halfway up the path, her gleaming hair flowing out behind her like Starlight's mane. It was a beautiful sight.

Champ ate up the ground in a mad dash to catch Starlight and by the time Caitlyn pulled up on the reins, halting her near the cabin, we were side by side. Her cheeks were flushed, and her eyes bright with the exhilaration of the ride.

"That felt wonderful," she called out to me.

"You never cease to amaze me, my Love," I called back. "You ride well."

Enjoying the feel of my horse, I suggested to Caitlyn that we ride back to the barn, saddle the horses, and then head up to the trails.

Accepting my offer, she turned the mare and called out, "Race ya," taking off again, giving Starlight free rein. I held Champ back just enough so I could stay behind her, watching while Caitlyn matched the gait of the horse as she rode. It was very impressive.

We spent the morning exploring the trails, laughing together, and enjoying our mutual pleasure of riding. When we returned to the barn Caitlyn went right to work, returning Starlight to her stall and brushing her down, the whole time murmuring to the mare about how beautiful she was. Starlight ate it up and nuzzled against Caitlyn showing her pleasure.

"I'll bring you a sweet carrot next time Starlight, for a sweet girl," I heard her soft words to the horse as I watched her reach for the shovel, intent on mucking out the stall.

"I'll get that Caitlyn," I told her as I walked towards her, my arm extended for the shovel.

"Excuse me Jacob, but I'm perfectly capable of shoveling out a little manure," she said, tilting her head forward, squinting her eyes, and giving me a look that caused her forehead to wrinkle. I couldn't help but laugh.

I stood there watching her as she mucked the stall, then spread fresh hay, and give Starlight her feed. Caitlyn had removed her jacket, pushing up her sleeves, giving me a view of her firm shape as she worked, and imagined how sexy she would look later in a warm tub of water. Looking up at me, and glancing down at the obvious sign of where my thoughts were, she asked, "Don't you have any work to do, Sir?"

Shaking my head, and laughing, I walked away reluctantly, and got to the chores that required my attention. Every so often I would glance around finding Caitlyn, who had finished with Starlight and was now exploring the barn. Whenever our eyes met we'd share a smile. Once I lost track of her, and after a moment of panic, I spotted her in the loft rummaging through the stuff stored up there. Finishing up, I joined her there.

Caitlyn had opened the shutter on the window to give her more light and I felt the wind gusting through. Looking out I could see the darkening sky. "We better head home Caitie-Lyn," I called to her.

Sadness flushed her face and her eyes filled with tears. Walking to her I asked, "What's wrong Love?"

"My sister calls me that," she answered, as her tears spilled down her cheeks. "I really miss her."

Taking her in my arms I apologized as another strong gust blew through the window.

"We need to get home before this sky opens up," I warned. Closing the shutter and latching it, I followed her down the steps. Before leaving I made sure the barn was secure, noting the presence of the chickens, aware now that we were in for another storm.

We made it to the cabin just as the icy rain started pelting the ground. Caitlyn was in a somber mood, I'm sure with a case of homesickness. I went upstairs and filled the tub, hoping that a warm bath would lift her spirits. When it was ready I went down to tell her and found her standing by the fireplace, staring at the fire.

Hearing me she turned, giving me a tentative smile. "I really miss my family Jacob, but I wouldn't give up one second of the time I've spent with you," she said.

With a feeling of relief I went to her, enveloping her in my embrace. Together we went upstairs and spent the afternoon lifting both our spirits.

Caitlyn

After a couple of weeks of stormy weather, the day dawned calm, with clear skies and bright sunlight, mild for this time of year. With no threat of an impending storm, Jacob suggested a trip to town to restock some much needed supplies. I was delighted with the prospect, wanting to see what town in 1882 was like.

Jacob headed to the barn to hook up the horses to the sled, while I got ready. By the time he returned I was dressed, I had chosen a modest outfit, of a skirt and blouse, that I prayed would look proper for an outing to town. "Do I look alright?" I questioned him, getting his nod of approval, and a lascivious look. Wearing the better of the warm coats I had I ran down the steps and jumped in, raring to go.

The trip to town was a feast for my photographer's eye, every corner we turned exposing beauty like nothing I'd ever seen. I was awed by the sun's rays, breaking through the leafless trees, adding sparkle to the snow and ice covering everything. My eyes darting from one place to the next, catching sight of little animals scurrying about in search of food they would need to get through the winter.

At one particularly beautiful spot Jacob stopped the sled. Reaching in his pocket he pulled out a thin gold band and handed it to me saying, "Put this on your finger, it'll keep the busy bodies in town quiet."

I had been wondering what the town folks would think about my sudden appearance, and thanked him for his thoughtfulness. I kind of enjoyed the idea of being Jacob's wife, even if it was just pretend.

Making a final turn I spotted the wooden town up ahead. It looked like something I had seen in movies depicting the era. We passed buildings, built side by side, with hand made signs advertising the businesses within. I could have easily spent a day walking around here with my camera.

We stopped in front of the General Store, and I couldn't believe it actually had a sign out front that read, "General Store." I let out a little giggle at the humor of it, catching Jacob's attention, which he rewarded with his smile. He helped me down and we went inside.

The inside was even better than the outside. There was close to a dozen customers milling about, probably taking advantage of the break in the stormy weather to do a little socializing, and were now casting curious glances my way.

Jacob led me to the clerk, greeting him with a hand shake and introducing me, "Marshall, I'd like you to meet my wife, Caitlyn. We were married in November on my last trip to the city. Pack up anything she thinks we need."

Marshall nodding his head to Jacob, turned to me and said, "Nice to meet you Caitlyn."

Nodding my head and smiling I reciprocated the greeting.

Jacob asked if I'd be alright for a while as he needed to make a stop at the Blacksmith's. I told him not to worry about me, shopping was my specialty. Kissing me on the cheek, he left the store. I could see the women in the shop, having heard the introductions, were now giving me little smiling nods, their heads together excited about this new tidbit of gossip they had to share.

Pulling my list out of my pocket, I started looking around at all the store shelves stacked with the staples needed for everyday life. Marshall followed along collecting the items as I found them. Stopping at the counter, I spotted a stack of large bars of chocolate. I had used the only one in the cabin pantry to make the cookies for Jacob's birthday, which he loved.

Marshall, noticing my eyes on the chocolate smiled at me, saying, "That's one of Jacob's favorites . . . he's been buying them for years." Delighted, I told him we'd take six.

By the time I was finished Jacob had returned, his smile devilish as he said, "Come with me, I have a surprise for you."

With a wave, he told Marshall we'd be back later to get our purchases, then putting his arm around my waist, led me down the decked walkway. When we got to the last building I was surprised to see it was a photographer's shop. Jacob opened the front door, holding it for me, and enthralled I walked in. Again Jacob made introductions, but this time to Hans, the photographer.

Hans was an older man, wide in girth, with a round smiling face. With his German accent he announced, "Jekob hez esked me to photograph de two of yuz for a beleted vedding picture." Jacob watched my face for my reaction, and smiled when I let out a delighted peal of laughter. While Hans was getting set up I looked around his studio fascinated by his "modern" equipment.

When he was ready Hans posed us, instructing me to smile sweetly. Jacob's discreet comment, "Sweet doesn't quite describe your wanton behavior in my bed, Madame," caused me to turn my head quickly looking at him instead of the camera, and both of us burst out laughing just as Hans snapped the picture. Apologizing, Hans declared he could take another, but Jacob assured him that the one he got was just right.

We left Hans' shop and walked back to the General Store to pick up our purchases, where I noticed an increase in the female customers waiting for our return to get another look at the mystery woman who had snatched up Jacob Wilkinson.

While Jacob was loading our supplies, I mentioned that since Christmas was coming I might need a couple more chocolate bars for cookie baking and with his enthusiastic nod of agreement I went back inside to purchase them. When I came back outside I was surprised to see this very beautiful, voluptuous woman, leaning intimately into

Jacob and whispering in his ear with a familiarity that sparked an instant territorial response in me.

Jacob spotted me heading directly for them and when our eyes met I could almost read the, "Ut-Oh!" in his mind. Trying to remove himself from her grasp Jacob stammered out, "Oh, there you are Sweetheart, I'd like you to meet my friend, umm acquaintance, Louisa."

"Friend Jacob? We are a bit more than friends," She murmured, looking at me with contempt.

Jacob finally snapped out of his daze and made the introduction, "Louisa, I'd like you to meet my wife, Caitlyn."

"Wife! When did you get married Jacob? You didn't mention anything about a wife in September when you were at my house," Louisa stated looking at me slyly, apparently going for my jugular with her words.

"Louise was it?" I asked questionably, knowing my error with her name would probably infuriate her. I knew I hit the mark when she turned her icy eyes on me.

"Louisa," she corrected, continuing with, "How long have you known her Jacob?" then turning to me she said, "He and I have been friends for a couple of years now, very close friends, if you know what I mean."

Moving between Louisa and Jacob and taking his arm, I gave her a contemptuous look and said, "Jacob, I've got this, Darling," reaching up with my hand and caressing his face.

Turning to her with challenge in my eyes I stated, "We've known each other most of our lives, and for at least the last ten years he's been so madly in love with me that he's tenaciously begged for my hand. I finally decided to put the poor man out of his misery and accept his proposal."

During this whole exchange Jacob had been standing there looking extremely uncomfortable. My last comment brought a slight smile to his face and he was at least smart enough to put his arm around my waist in a possessive manner.

I decided it was time to end this conversation and stated loudly enough for all to hear, "Louise-ah, Jacob won't be visiting your home anymore. I'm very demanding of his time, and talents, he'll be way to busy, and exhausted to be making any house calls to you."

With that I turned and started walking towards the sled, calling over my shoulder, "Jacob are you coming?"

I heard him blurt out a quick, "Good Day Louisa," and then catch up to me, again circling my waist with his arm.

When we reached the sled he helped me in, looking a bit sheepish. I gave him a coquettish look, making sure Louisa saw it, and watched as she stormed off in a huff. I also noticed that the gossips were going wild, casting me looks of satisfaction. This had probably been the most excitement they'd had around here in years.

We headed for home in the supply laden sled, the afternoon sleigh ride back starting out in silence. When we were about half way home Jacob finally decided to say something.

"I'm sorry about that Caitlyn, I was hoping to avoid running into her."

"She better avoid me, I wanted to rip the bitches eyes out," I said venomously. "How dare she throw your past relationship in my face like that. The thought of you making love to another woman doesn't sit well with me Jacob."

"Caitlyn, I've never made love to any woman but you. I might have had sex, but there was never any love involved," he told me, being honest.

"Is there anyone else in town I need to avoid?" I asked him.

"No Love, and I don't think you'll have any more problems with Louisa, you managed to put her in her place quite well," he said with pride in his voice.

"I don't like being jealous Jacob, and I have no intentions of sharing you with anyone. I hope I made that abundantly clear to everyone, especially you."

"Crystal clear, Baby," he said, pulling me up against his side as we continued our journey home.

Jacob was mine now, so I put Louisa out of my mind, and concentrated on the man beside me, and the beauty around me. Snuggling closer, I felt his arm tighten around me. Looking up at his handsome face, he bent his head and kissed me with passion.

When he pulled back I looked in his eyes and said, "If it wasn't so damn cold I'd be demanding some of your talents right here Sir."

Jacob snapped the reins and got the horses moving faster, giving me that smile of his that let me know we were on the same wave length.

Jacob

While enjoying breakfast with Caitlyn, I let her know about my plans to go meet with Samuel this morning. She informed me that her plans including baking the most exquisite Apple Pie I've ever seen. Knowing how talented she was in the kitchen, I was sure she was right. She was putting all the food supplies, from our trip to town a week ago, to good use.

Before leaving for the barn I asked, "If Hattie Mae extends an invitation for dinner, should I accept?"

"Of course, I'm dying to meet them, besides I'd love a little female company for a change," she informed me. "It's not that I don't love your company, I really do, it's just that women are different." She really didn't have to tell me this fact, in truth it was like the two sexes were from totally different planets.

When I got to the Williams' home the first thing Hattie asked was, "When you gonna bring that girl over for me to meet, Jacob?"

"Are you inviting?" I asked her.

"Yes I am, you come on back with Caitlyn later and I'll fix you both a fine supper."

"Sounds great Hattie, we'll be here," I promised.

When I got back home Caitlyn had two, just in case we received an invite, of the most beautiful Apple Pies I'd truly ever seen, sitting on the counter cooling. The centers had a crisp topping and around the edged she had made leaf shapes out of the crust that were sprinkled with sugar and baked golden brown. They really were exquisite pies.

When I told her about the invitation she was ecstatic, requesting that I heat up some water so she could bathe. I agreed if she'd allow me to join her.

While we sat in the tub, Caitlyn scrubbing my back, she leaned forward over my shoulder, her breasts rubbing against me, and said, "Tell me about Samuel and Hattie Mae, Jacob."

At that moment the only thing I could think about were her breasts and I told her, "Madame, if you want me to use my brain you'll have to remove your bosoms from my back."

Laughing, she stood partially up and slid them up my back until they were positioned on each side of my neck. "Is this better?" she asked coyly. Grabbing her, I spun her around to my lap, and we spent the next 30 minutes doing other things besides talking.

When we were both out of the tub, and dressed, she asked me about our dinner hosts again. Sitting together on the couch I told her some of their story.

"My parents bought a small part of this farm in 1848, just after they were married, about 200 acres and the old cabin that Samuel and Hattie live in now," I started. "It was pretty rough for them in the beginning, the first Winter almost sent them running, but they stuck it out."

I had Caitlyn's rapt attention so I continued, "One night in the Winter of 1849 my parent's dogs heard a disturbance out in the old barn, my father thought it might be wolves after the livestock, so he went out with his rifle to investigate, ready to take care of the problem."

"When he got to the barn he looked down his rifle at four Negroes; Samuel, Hattie Mae and their two young sons, terrified of the dogs, and hiding in the barn. Samuel begged my father not to hurt his family, and apologized for coming on his property, but said he had to find shelter for his son, who was real sick."

Turning to Caitlyn I said, "My father was a compassionate man, and he could see that the boy was sick. Feeling his forehead he knew the young child needed help, or he probably wouldn't make it. He told them to follow him, and brought them into the cabin, and to my mother."

Caitlyn's eyes filled with tears as she imagined the fear that Samuel and Hattie Mae must have been feeling, and the blessing, that they had ended up in Jacob's parents barn.

I knew the story by heart because Hattie Mae had told it to me many times over the years, so I went on, "My mother took Isaac from Hattie Mae, and tucked him into her own bed. Getting rags she dipped them in cold water, and laid them on the boy's head in an attempt to lower his fever."

"Turning over the task to Hattie, my mother went to the kitchen and heated them all some soup, knowing it was important to try to get some nourishment into the sick boy, and truthfully into the whole family. Hattie managed to spoon feed a small amount to Isaac, and he fell asleep in the warm bed."

"Hattie tried to move her son out of the bed and my mother told her to just leave him be. She made sure that all of them ate their fill, and giving them blankets, told them they could sleep near their son. By the next morning Isaac's temperature was down, and he was able to eat some toast."

"Thanking my father for his kindness, Samuel felt he owned him the truth, and told my father that they were run-away slaves, that their master had intended on selling him, and separate him from his family, so they had escaped. Samuel went on to explain that he had seen what had happened to his own mother when the same thing happened to his Daddy, and he wouldn't allow it to happen to Hattie Mae because he loved her too much."

Looking over at Caitlyn, I could see that she was caught up in the story, her eyes showing her emotions, were tear filled, and she begged, "Please go on Jacob."

"My father and mother asked them to stay, told them that they could use their help with the farm, and in return they would keep them safe from their past. At first they lived in the barn, making part of it a comfortable temporary home. Samuel, with my father's help, built a small cabin for them and by the Winter of 1850 they were moved in."

"Our farm was flourishing and my father was able to buy 300 more acres. Samuel's knowledge of the plantation down south made him an irreplaceable asset. My father always believed that if it hadn't been for Samuel he would have gone under. They became friends, not boss and employee, colleagues. Working together they both prospered."

"And my mother and Hattie Mae bonded like sisters. If Hattie Mae hadn't been here the day I was born my mother and I probably would have died during childbirth, but Caitlyn, I'm going to save that story for Hattie to tell you, because we have to get going or we'll be late for dinner," I informed her, getting up to leave.

She jumped up from the couch, not realizing how late it was getting, and got herself ready. When I told her I'd go for the sled, she told me she'd rather just walk to the barn for a little exercise. Putting on our coats, Caitlyn grabbed one of her pies, and I grabbed my rifle, explaining that it might be getting close to dark when we'd be heading home.

The 30 minute sleigh ride was fun for both of us, Caitlyn enjoyed all the new sights she'd never seen on this side of the farm, and I enjoyed the sight of Caitlyn. When we arrived I helped her out of the sled and before we could make it to the door Hattie Mae came rushing out the door of the cabin to greet us.

"Oh, here you are, just look at you, such a pretty thing," Hattie Mae fawned over Caitlyn. "Jacob why don't you go on down to the barn and see what Samuel and the boys are up to, while Miss Caitlyn and I get acquainted," she said, dismissing me, and putting her arm around Caitlyn leading her into their cabin.

"It's nice to see you again too, Hattie Mae," I said as she closed the cabin door in my face.

Caitlyn

"It's so nice to finally meet you, Mrs. Williams," I began, handing Hattie Mae the Apple Pie.

"You call me Hattie Mae, child, everyone does. Oh my, what a pretty pie," Hattie exclaimed as she helped me off with my coat and led me to the table to sit. "Can I get you a cup of tea to warm you up?"

"That would be lovely, Hattie Mae."

When Hattie had the tea ready she brought in two cups and joined me at the table. She sat across from me, a big smile on her face, just looking at me for a couple of minutes, then said, "I've been just dyin to meet the little lady who stole Jacob's heart."

"Hattie, Jacob is wonderful, and he's stolen my heart too, but I'm just so happy to see you and hear another woman's voice," I told her. "I've really missed female company."

"Child, I know what you mean, yes I sure do." She went on, "I have my two daughters-in-law that live close by now so it's not so bad anymore, but when I first got here, it was just me and Miss Kathryn." "She was a pretty little thing, too, just like you. I can see, like father, like son," she said with a chuckle.

Hattie had a motherly way about her that made me feel instantly comfortable, and after just a few minutes we had formed a camaraderie, the two of us chatting back and forth like old friends. I totally understood why Jacob loved her so much.

"Hattie, Jacob tells me you helped with his birth, and that he and his mother probably wouldn't have made it if it wasn't for you," I stated. "I'd love to hear the whole story if you don't mind."

Standing up and heading to the kitchen, Hattie said cheerfully, "You come on over here with me and I'll talk while I finish up my cookin."

Following her I said, "If you've got an extra apron, I'd love to help." Smiling, Hattie handed me one, and standing side by side, mixing up the ingredients for biscuits, Hattie started the tale.

"Oh, it was cold that day, a storm was blowin in and by that night the winds were a howlin," Hattie began. "I was asleep in my bed when I heard that poor child's screams." "I woke up Samuel and told him I had to get to Miss Kat, that she needed me." "We got dressed and headed to this here cabin, and met Mr. Jake half way, scared to death, on his way to fetch me."

I was so engrossed in her story that I had stopped mixing and Hattie reminded me that we wouldn't be having any biscuits if I didn't get the batter ready. Apologizing, I continued kneading the dough, begging her to go on.

"When I got to Miss Kat she was in real bad shape, she had been havin them pains all day and hadn't told no one. I shoed the men out of the room and started to check her just as another pain hit her." Shaking her head with the memory, Hattie went on, "I felt that boy's foot and knew right away he was all twisted up in there and comin out the wrong way."

"I started sweet talkin Miss Kat, trying to soothe her, but really I was scared out of my wits. I had seen this before, but I wasn't the one helpin with the birthin." "I'll never forget Miss Kat's eyes looking at me all scared, and beggin me to help her." Tears filled Hattie's eyes remembering her friend's terror.

"When her pain eased off, I told Miss Kat what I had do, that I had to turn her baby around, sayin I was real sorry, that it was gonna hurt bad." "Another pain was comin fast and she grabbed my arm and screamed at me, 'Just do it, Hattie, save my baby.' I waited for the pain to pass and I put my hands in there and turned that baby around, Miss Kat screamin in pain the whole time."

"When the next pain came that poor child pushed real hard, and I saw the top of Jacob's little head. After a few more pains and lots of pushin by Miss Kat, I was holdin that boy in my hands, thankin the good Lord for his help."

I hadn't remembered doing it, but the biscuits were all made and on a tray ready for the oven. Hattie smiled at me, and finished the story.

"I cleaned that baby up and wrapped him up tight in a blanket, showin him to his worn out momma, then layin him in the cradle that Mr. Jake had made. Pushin his little fist to his mouth, he went right to sleep.

I got Miss Kat all cleaned up and comfortable and she grabbed my hand, and says to me, 'Thank you Hattie, I couldn't have done it without your help. I love you dearly friend.' I felt proud of me, Miss Caitlyn, for the first time in my whole life."

"When I went and got Mr. Jake to come see his boy, he came runnin in and went right to his sleepin wife, lookin at me all scared, I told him she was gonna be just fine, she was just tuckered out and needed her sleep. He gave me a big ole bear hug and then went over and just stood there, staring at his son. He was so proud of them both, it just warmed my heart."

"You know, a couple months later Mr. Jake gave me and Samuel our freedom papers. He had paid off our debt to the Master down south and we didn't have to worry bout him no more. When Samuel said he'd pay him back, Mr. Jake told him he'd never be able to repay me and Samuel for all we had done for him and Miss Kat. I coulda told him we felt the same."

It wasn't long after that when Jacob and Samuel returned from the barn, and came into the cabin finding us laughing and talking in the kitchen. After giving his wife a kiss on the cheek, Hattie introduced

Samuel to me. They had an easy loving relationship and it showed in their faces.

Isaac and Henry arrived with their wives and children and before long we were all sitting around the big table enjoying a happy family dinner. I glanced across the table and caught Jacob watching me, and gave him a joy filled smile that wasn't missed by Hattie.

After dessert, my pie getting rave reviews, Jacob and I headed home, promising to come back soon. The ride home together was shared in companionable silence until Jacob said, "I don't have to ask if you enjoyed yourself, it shows on your face."

"I had a wonderful time, they just envelop you into the family. I can't wait to spend time with them again," I told him.

Arriving at the barn we quickly took care of the animals, then headed to the cabin hand in hand, the pleasurable feelings of the day continuing. I was already planning in my mind, ways to continue these feelings into the night.

Jacob

The week before Christmas was an exciting time for me and Caitlyn, with both of us looking forward to spending our first Christmas together. Hattie Mae and Samuel had tried to convince us when we were at their home to join their family for the holiday, but we told them we really wanted to spend this special day alone. They seemed to understand how we felt, smiling at each other, as they had watched us leave.

Light snow had been falling for the past couple of days coating everything in a delicate covering of sparkling white. The light breeze was frigid, but when I suggested to Caitlyn that we should go out and look for a tree to decorate, her face lit up with delight at the idea. We bundled up, and walked down to the barn to hook up the big sled, and headed off on our mission, the dogs following along. The woods surrounding the farm were full of trees, suitable for our plans, and it didn't take us long to find the perfect one.

Hauling the tree back to the cabin, I carried it in and leaned it against the wall. Asking Caitlyn to come with me, we went up to the attic to hunt for the decorations and tree stand I knew were stored up there.

While rummaging around, I noticed a trunk that had belonged to my mother, that I had totally forgotten about, and decided I would come back up later to go through it, knowing I'd be able to find something in there that I could give Caitlyn for Christmas.

We located the decorations, and the stand my father had made, and after a couple of trips, back and forth, had everything in the living room ready to start. Caitlyn's childlike excitement was contagious as she went through the ornaments, expressing her glee when she found one she especially liked, while I got the tree secure in the stand.

After watching all the action for a while, Bear and Griz found comfortable spots and went to sleep. Thankfully not right under the tree.

Pausing for a few minutes before starting, Caitlyn ran into the kitchen to fix us both a mug of steaming hot chocolate to enjoy while we decorated. She said this was a family tradition that she insisted on keeping. It was alright with me, being the chocolate lover that I was.

Starting at the top, with the garland that my mother had made, I followed Caitlyns instructions as to where it should be placed. I could tell she was meticulous like my mother when it came to decorating, and the memories of my father, being ordered about by my mother while working on the tree, filled me with nostalgia. I truly missed them, especially during the holidays.

Once I got the top portion done to Caitlyn's specifications, she took over, draping the garland just so, while I held the strand to ease her progress. I think we worked really well as a team, and the garland was done in a matter of minutes. Standing back to survey her work, Caitlyn gave it a thumbs up. A quick kiss for me, and on to the ornaments.

Caitlyn was just as picky about the placement of the ornaments as she had been with the garland. I decided it was best for me to just hand them to her, and let her position them where she wanted. When she was done, no matter which side of the tree you looked at, it was beautiful.

After another, little longer kiss for me, Caitlyn started going through another box of decoration that my mother used to place around the room. When she was finished the whole room was filled with the fresh scent of pine, and the holiday spirit.

While Caitlyn sat and relaxed, admiring her work, I picked up all the empty boxes and returned them to the attic, taking the opportunity to go through the trunk while I was up there. I found the two sapphire and diamond hair combs that I was looking for, and put them aside so I could get to them easily. Caitlyn was going to love them.

When I got back downstairs, my Christmas present, and the prettiest decoration in the cabin, was sound asleep on the couch.

Caitlyn

Waking up after my impromptu nap, I looked around at the living room filled with the Christmas decorations, and the magnificent smelling tree. It looked so beautiful that I longed for my camera again. The warmth of the rustic cabin setting, with the touches of Christmas decor, would have made a top selling card cover.

Letting my eyes scan the room, they rested on Jacob sitting comfortably in his chair reading a book. He seemed to be absorbed in what he was reading so I just laid there watching him for a minute. I loved looking at him, he was so handsome. Powerfully built, a real mountain man type, but intelligent and sophisticated too. He would have fit in at ease anywhere, and I pictured him dressed in a Tux, with me all dressed to the nines, at some formal get together, the two of us making a rather attractive-looking couple.

Coming out of my reverie with the sound of the clock bonging 1:00 p.m., I found his eyes on me and couldn't help smiling. Setting his book down, he rose from his chair and came to me.

Sitting up and making room for him to join me, he sat down and pulled me up against his side. I realized then that there was no place I'd rather be than right here, alone with him, instead of at some fancy party.

"Did you have a nice nap?" he asked.

"Very nice, thank you," I answered, cuddling closer to him. "I guess decorating wore me out." "Did you have lunch?" I asked.

"No, I just grabbed a slab of that pound cake you made yesterday, I didn't know what you were planning for dinner and I didn't want you shrieking at me for ruining your plans," he informed me with a smirk.

"I don't shriek, Jacob."

"I bet I could make you shriek, if you'll let me try," he said, sliding the back of his hand down the side of my breast.

Enjoying the touch of his hand for just a minute before getting up, I told him, "Maybe later, I'm starving right now." Bending over and giving him a kiss, I headed for the kitchen.

Following behind me, he was all hands, as he asked, "You'd deny a starving man what he needs most?"

"I'd never deny you, my Love, but right now I need some sustenance to give me the energy I'll need to keep up with your enticing offer." My response seemed to please him and he agreed that we could both use some food to get us through his rigorous plans for the afternoon.

While we were eating lunch he pointed to the small table in the living room and said, "While I was in the attic I found a few things that we can use to amuse ourselves while we're snowed in."

Looking over, I spotted a Chess set, a couple of decks of cards, and a wooden, brief case like, box. Forgetting about my lunch for the moment, I headed over to the table to check out the simple forms of entertainment that filled me with enthusiasm.

Picking up a deck of cards, I did a little fancy shuffling, and said, "I hope you have lots of money sir, your gonna need it if you plan on sitting across from me at the poker table."

Laughing, he shook his head, and looking at me with challenge in his eyes, stated, "Women's brains are not as calculating as men's when it comes to gaming, little lady."

Letting out a loud "Ha," I dared, "Maybe you'd like to put a little wager on that," Mister."

"Name your price Madame, no wait, I have a better idea," he bantered back, a conniving look in his eyes, "We'll just play for the shirt on your back, so to speak."

"Finish your lunch and then we'll see who's sitting around the table shirtless," I said, accepting his challenge.

We were silent as we finished eating, both of us sizing the other up with cunning eyes while scheming out our individual strategies. I thought to myself that distraction techniques would probably be my best bet, since I really didn't know how good a poker player he was. I did, however, know how easily I could distract Jacob's mind with my purposefully placed tongue, and I was planning on playing dirty.

After clearing the table and putting away all the lunch stuff, we took our seats across the table from each other. Jacob winning the split, he dealt first. I could tell from the way he handled the cards that he'd done this before, probably quite a bit.

He won the first hand fair and square, my cards were terrible, so I removed the ribbon from the end of my braid and handed it to him. I got his raised eyebrow for this.

When he won the second hand I untied one of my shoes and provocatively kicked it away from the table.

The next three hands were mine and I got both his shoes, and one sock, leaving him with only four more articles of clothing to loose before being completely naked. Perhaps I should have mentioned the fact that he was wearing a lot fewer items than me before we had started playing.

He won the next five hands, which lost me my other shoe, both socks, my blouse and skirt, leaving me in a precarious position. It was time to pull out the big guns.

After dealing the cards, and scrutinizing his hand, he asked, "How many do you want Caitlyn?"

Pretending to contemplate my cards, and his question, I let my tongue glide slowly across my upper lip, before softly saying, "three." When I glanced up at him, waiting for my cards, I saw his attention on my mouth as he swallowed hard.

When I showed my winning hand, he looked at me with narrowed eyes, and said, "Your cheating Caitlyn."

"I have no idea what your talking about Jacob." I said, giving him a wily look.

Deciding to give me a taste of my own medicine, he slid back from the table a little and slowly removed his shirt, exposing his muscular chest and shoulders, and his firm abs. It was my turn to gulp as I felt that throbbing in my lower regions again. When I lost the next hand, to his bluff, I knew I was in trouble.

Standing up I removed my petticoat, leaving me in only my sheer chemise since I found the long under pants that women wore in the 1800's cumbersome and often went without.

Jacob stood up and came to me, his desire full blown, he said, "You win Caitlyn," as he lifted me quickly from my chair and carried me to the nearest flat surface, giving me my victory prize.

Jacob

After the day of our rousing Poker tournament, Caitlyn and I enjoyed playing some very interesting games of Chess. I tried to convince her that Strip Chess would be the most entertaining, but she refused, telling me it was too distracting for a game like Chess. She was very good at the game and took great pleasure in kicking my ass with her Queen as often as possible.

The thing Caitlyn was the most thrilled about was the set of oil paints that my father had bought for my mother. I found a couple of blank canvases for her and she took them upstairs to one of the smaller bedrooms, hiding up there for hours working on something that she said was a surprise.

It snowed hard for the last couple of days before Christmas, but on Christmas Eve it slowed enough for Caitlyn and I to make a quick trip to Samuel and Hattie Mae's to wish them a happy holiday.

Caitlyn had loaded up the sled with all kinds of delicious cookies, and a pecan pie she had baked especially for Hattie, knowing from their last visit that it was a favorite of hers. While I spent the time discussing plans for the spring planting with Samuel, I watched the two ladies, their heads together, laughing, and talking, about whatever it is women talk about.

When we noticed the snowfall increasing Caitlyn and I said our goodbyes, and Merry Christmases, and headed back to the cabin, Bear and Griz bounding around the sled all the way home.

Building up the fire for our evening of cuddling on the couch, I waited for Caitlyn to join me. I had noticed during dinner that she was in a pensive mood and when we sat together I asked what was on her mind.

"I'm just thinking about my family, this is the first Christmas I've ever spent without them," she answered.

"What did your family usually do on Christmas Eve?" I inquired, hoping it wouldn't make her sad thinking about it.

"We always had a wonderful family dinner, my mother took turns making one of our favorite meals each year, then most times we would stay up late and go to Midnight Mass. It wasn't so much the what we did, it was just being together. I have a wonderful family Jacob, I wish you could meet them."

"I feel like I should apologize for taking you away from them, but truthfully, I'm not at all sorry that you're here with me instead," I told her honestly.

"I'm not sorry either, Jacob," she told me, then bringing her lips to mine, she kissed me deeply.

This was going to my best Christmas ever, and I hoped I'd be able to make it hers too. We sat together, watching the crackling fire, just enjoying the companionship of each other. After about an hour of this peace, I hugged her closer to me, thinking she had fallen asleep.

Hearing her sigh, I wrapped her in my arms and was rewarded when she said, "Make love to me Jacob, I need to feel you."

I got up and moved the screen in front of the fireplace, then returned to her, extending my hand. She rose and we walked upstairs arm in arm. We spent the next couple of hours filling both our needs.

Caitlyn

Christmas morning dawned bright and sunny. Sometime during the night the snow had stopped falling and now the early sunlight was shining in the windows lighting up the cabin with a warm glow. I felt like a kid, there was just something about Christmas that brought the child out in me.

Jacob was still asleep next to me, but when I tried to get out of bed he tightened his grip, holding my body next to his much warmer one. Since there was no time limits on the day, I decided to stay where I was, and just enjoy the feel of his comforting embrace.

After about a half hour, my excitement, and my hunger, couldn't be contained. When my stomach gave a loud growl, Jacob finally loosened his hold on me and asked, "Are you hungry, Love?"

"Starving," I answered, as I climbed out of bed, naked. "You and I burned a lot of calories last night. I feel like I eat twice as much food as I used to, but haven't gained an ounce."

Looking over my bare body with attentive eye, he pronounced, "Your body is as fine as it was the first time I saw it, maybe even finer."

Giving him a smile, I thanked him for his compliment, and headed into the bathroom. When I came out he was sitting on the side of the bed stretching, causing me to pause and admire the view.

Seeing me looking at him, he patted the bed next to him, giving me his most tempting come hither look. Knowing if I got within arms length of him I'd never get out of the room, I wagged my finger at him, and grabbed my robe, making a quick get away so I could get our breakfast ready.

When he joined me downstairs about 15 minutes later, I had the coffee ready and half a platter full of Apple Cinnamon Crunch Pancakes, the first thing I had ever cooked for him. Seeing them, he gave a big smile of approval at my choice for our first Christmas breakfast together, and sat down at the table to wait for me to finish up and join him.

After taking two on my plate, I watched as Jacob grabbed a stack of six large pancakes, and topping them with a little Maple Syrup, started attacking them like a starving man, stopping only long enough to wash them down occasionally with a gulp of coffee.

Deciding if I wanted any more, I better grab a couple before he ate them all. I got them on my plate just in time for him to ask, "Do you want any more?"

With my negative headshake, he cleaned off the rest of the platter. It really was a pleasure to watch someone enjoying your cooking with such gusto. Getting up from the table, I noticed a slight bulge in his usually flat abs, and couldn't help giving his stomach a little pat, as I walked past him with the empty platter.

"Your trying to make me fat woman," he stated with a satiated smile. "Maybe next time you should only make half as many," he suggested as he helped me clear the table.

"Then what will I eat?" I asked, joking with him, and getting his easy laughter as a reward for my drollness.

After finishing in the kitchen, quickly with his help, we refilled our mugs with coffee and moved out into the living room near the Christmas tree.

"I've got something for you Caitlyn," he told me, running up the stairs and saying, "I'll be right back."

When he returned he handed me a present wrapped in a beautiful lace handkerchief. Opening it I found two hair combs, sparkling with sapphires and diamonds, each in the shape of half of a butterfly's wings. They were so beautiful, and when inserted on each side of my braid they would form a dazzling butterfly on the back of my head.

"The sapphires are the same color as your mesmerizing eyes," he told me, looking into mine with all the love he was feeling.

I was so pleased by his gift I moved automatically to his body and wrapped my arms around him, saying, "Thank you Jacob, I love them," and then raised up for a lingering kiss.

"I want you to wear them for me later, just the combs," he informed me smiling.

"Sounds good to me," I told him, then remembering my present for him, I told him I'd be back in a minute, and ran up to get it. Coming back down and handing it to him, I explained, "It's not as nice as the combs but it means a lot to me, I hope you like it."

Unwrapping the canvas, Jacob looked at the oil painting of the twin trees in the valley. Never having used oils before, I was quite pleased with the results and hoped he liked it too.

"Wow Caitlyn, I didn't know you could paint," he said, showing his amazement, and making me feel proud of my artistic ability. "I can even see the opening of the cave on the rock face. It's really good."

"Thank you, Jacob. The first time I ever saw you, you were standing right there," I said, pointing to the tree on the right, "You were leaning against that tree with your arms crossed, and a really sexy smile on your face," I finished.

"I went through those trees hundreds of times over the past 22 years, to come see you," he told me, reminiscing. "I really love the picture, and you."

The rest of our first Christmas was spent in blissful happiness. We went down to the barn in the late afternoon, walking hand in hand, with Bear and Griz doing their bouncing, romping thing all the way there. On the way back to the cabin the snow started falling again, ending the brightness of the day with swirling flurries.

We enjoyed my world famous Beef Stew and biscuits for dinner, and since I had made the stew a couple of days prior, the prep for the meal was easy. The whole day had been tranquil and enjoyable, followed by an evening of relaxation, beginning with a long soak in the hot tub.

After our bath Jacob left the bathroom first giving me enough time to slip the Butterfly combs into my hair. Walking out into the bedroom and doing a slow turn for him, wearing only the combs as he had requested, I was rewarded with his passionate look of appreciation.

"The way you look right now is burned in the memories of my soul, Caitlyn," he said, his voice husky with emotion.

Our lovemaking was tender and unhurried, both of us giving and receiving pleasure from the others touch. I had never felt so complete, and knew in my heart Jacob felt it to. I fell asleep in his embrace, as close as two people could ever be, in both body, and spirit.

Jacob

My first Christmas with Caitlyn was the most pleasurable experience of my life. I never realized that the connection between us would be so powerful. She was my heart, and soul. I wanted to have a lifetime of Christmases with her, and every other holiday, in the years to come.

Whenever I thought about Spring, which was always right there in the back of my mind, I knew I wouldn't be able to just let her go. I needed her as much as I wanted her, and with only three, possibly four months to convince her to stay with me, I intended to do everything in my power to accomplish it.

Thinking about our lovemaking last night, I smiled to myself. I had made her shriek, she told me she didn't shriek but she most definitely had last night. She also moaned, gasped and begged. Her body was so responsive to my touch and I took great pleasure in bringing her right to the edge and then slowing it back down, making her needs intense.

This was part of my strategy to keep her here. I was going to make her body want me so much that she would never consider walking away, and I intended to continue even if it killed me. Chuckling to myself, I thought, "Oh, what a way to go."

Finishing up in the barn, I grabbed the basket of eggs Caitlyn had asked me to get while I was here, and headed back to the cabin, whistling for the dogs to follow. Thinking about my next plan of attack during the walk back had me all worked up by the time I got there. Unfortunately Caitlyn was elbow deep in flour, and gave me a, "what took you so long" look.

Setting the eggs on the counter, I made a hasty retreat to the table, sitting to hide where my very obvious thoughts had been. Trying to get myself under control, I asked if there was anything she needed help with, and got her usual, "I've got everything under control," response. That made at least one of us, I thought.

I watched her as she dropped blobs of raisin filled dough onto the cookie sheet she used daily, wondering what delicious creation those blobs were going to become. She slid them into the oven and began cleaning up her work area, being meticulous about the cleanliness of her kitchen.

She seemed to prefer that I keep out of, what she considered, her part of the cabin. No complaints here, as long as I got to eat whatever she made in there I was happy. After about 30 minutes she had everything cleaned up, and pulled the pan out of the oven revealing golden brown buns that had plumped up to twice their original size. The enticing aroma filling the whole cabin.

She moved the buns to a wire rack and drizzled them with a sugary glaze. Putting on a pot of coffee to brew while she washed the pan. When the coffee was ready she carried the rack of buns to the table and poured us each a cup. Sitting down, she smiled at me and asked, "Would you like to try a Golden Raisin Bun?"

With the nod of my head, she put one on the plate in front of me, also giving herself one. Picking it up, I took a big bite of heaven. My God they were delicious, still warm, soft and eggy inside, the raisins and glaze just the right amount of sweetness. I polished it off in three bites, and grabbed another. By the time I left the table I had eaten four.

The dogs, standing by patiently and drooling all over the floor in hopes of getting a treat, were disappointed when Caitlyn said, "Sorry boys, no raisins for dogs."

"Why not?" I asked her, still licking the glaze off my fingers.

"They're toxic to dogs, same with onions and chocolate," she informed me. "It can kill them if they eat too much," she finished, pulling out a couple of small pieces of bacon, from breakfast, and giving each dog one.

"That's good to know. It's amazing how much knowledge you have stored in that pretty little head of yours," I told her.

As I watched, she gave the dogs a pointed finger command, without saying a word, and they obediently went into the living room and laid down. They listened to her better than they ever did for me, and she didn't even have to say anything. I also realized that if she had pointed for me to go lay down, I would have done it too. It was amazing how she made us males eager to please.

Caitlyn

New Years eve had dawned clear and cold, and by nighttime the sky was still snow free and bright. The full moon cast a glow on the mountaintops turning them into a silhouette against the star filled sky. Jacob and I, bundled up in our warm coats, stood out on the porch taking in the splendor of our surroundings. The untarnished wilderness had a stark beauty that invaded the soul causing it to become a part of you. I truly understood why Jacob loved it here.

Standing together, looking out at the mountains with his arms wrapped around me, we heard the Grandfather clock begin the 12 chimes that would herald in the New Year. With the final bong Jacob tightened his grip and whispered in my ear, "Happy New Year my Love."

Turning in his arms, I tilted my head back and looked into his eyes, sincerely responding with, "Happy New Year to you too, Jacob," then standing on my toes I met him half way for our first kiss of 1883, the first of many I hoped.

We continued standing there looking up at the stars, both of us spotting one shooting across the sky at he same time. My wish, that our love would last forever. Jacob didn't share his wish out loud, but from the look in his eyes I'm pretty sure it mirrored mine.

Jacob

The sound of the howling winds and the snow pelting the shuttered windows brought me out of my peaceful slumber wrapped around Caitlyn's soft warm body. After the past couple of days of mild weather this storm arrived unexpectedly in the early morning hours bringing the heavy snow and high winds that made the world outside seem like total chaos.

I hated the thought of moving from the tranquility of holding her, to the journey I had to make out to the barn to insure the animals were safe and protected. As I moved to rise Caitlyn stirred and looked at me with those eyes of hers. God she could make me forget about everything in the world except her.

"Where are you going?" she asked as she stretched and yawned awake.

"I've got to get to the barn to make sure the animals are okay," I told her smiling.

"In this?" she asked coming fully awake, concern changing her eyes to an even darker shade of blue. "Can't you wait just a little while? Maybe the winds will die down a bit."

"From the racket this storm is making it's going to be a long time before there's any calming down," I told her pulling on my pants and getting dressed in as many layers of clothing as possible while still being able to move. I could judge from the chill in the room that the temp had dipped below zero outside, and freezing to death was not on my "Things To Do Today" list. I walked over to the wood stove and added a log to warm the room.

Caitlyn climbed out of bed, wrapping herself in her heavy robe as she followed closely behind me down the stairs. "Let me put on the coffee . . . something to warm your insides before you go out," she said with a nervous smile, trying to stall my departure.

"I'll need it more when I get back," I called over my shoulder as I headed to the bench by the door to put on my boots. "It shouldn't take me more than an hour," I said to her as the Grandfather clock began chiming out eight bongs. "I'll take Griz with me, Bear will stay here with you."

I finished lacing up my boots, strapped on my snow shoes, and stood. She rushed to me trying to wrap her arms around the added bulk of my clothing in an attempt to stop me from leaving.

"I'll be back in an hour," I told her reassuringly as I hugged her to me. "I'm going to be hungry when I get back, so get breakfast ready woman," I joked, kissing her, then turning to open the door. "Stay inside, latch this door behind me, and keep it closed until you hear me come back."

Hooking the leash to Griz's collar I opened the door. A gust of wind caught it, almost ripping it out of my hands, but I managed to hold it firm letting Griz out behind me.

Making my way down the stairs and to the path leading to the barn was rough but I knew once I was on the path, and as long as I didn't hit any trees, I would eventually end up at the barn. My father and I had cleared the path this way so when the weather was like it is today you could still get to the barn without getting disorientated and lost.

Leaning into the wind and letting Griz pull me along behind him by the leash helped me reach my destination sooner than I expected. As I approached the barn I noticed the large build-up of snow on the roof, knowing that I would have to get up there as soon as it stopped, and clear it off to keep it from collapsing.

Entering the barn I pulled the door closed behind me holding on tightly so it wouldn't get wrenched from my hands and damaged by the wind.

Latching it I got right to work, knowing that as soon as I was done I could get back inside and warm up with Caitlyn.

The calm inside the barn was quite a contrast from the turbulence outside. I began checking to make sure all window shutters were closed so that the barn was secured. Seeing one flapping back and forth in the upper deck I headed up with my tools and found that the latch had been broken by the high winds. After getting it closed I nailed it shut then braced it with a piece of wood.

I headed to the horses, throwing blankets over all four and spreading out fresh hay, then filled their buckets with feed. Checking the water barrels I found that they hadn't froze solid so that wasn't a problem for now. I moved to the cows following pretty much the same routine. The Chickens had found their warm spot in the barn to roost and would be safe until the storm passed, so all I had left to do was give them some feed and head back home to my warm little Caitlyn, I thought with a smile.

When I opened the door to leave, holding it for Griz to join me, a strong gust caught it, wrenching it out of my hands and slamming it into the wall of the barn. The force of the door flung me to the ground a few feet in front of it just as the snow from the roof came tumbling down on top of me.

Thinking quickly I rolled to my stomach and managed to bring my hands up to protect my face, fanning my bent arms back and forth to form a pocket of air around my head so I would be able to breath, at least for a little while. The weight of the heavy snow pinned me to the ground making movement impossible. I was in trouble. I laid there, my mind going to Caitlyn. I finally had her with me and now I could die. "God, what did I do to deserve this?"

I started to drift off when I heard the faint sound of barking. "That's it Griz, you get me out boy," was the last thought I had before I passed out.

Caitlyn

Waiting in the cabin was agonizing. I kept checking the slow moving time on the Grandfather clock, so far only 10 minutes had passed, and I tried willing it to move more swiftly. When Jacob had informed me of his intention to go out in this dangerous storm my intuition kicked in leaving me with an intense feeling of dread.

I begged him to wait, hoping for some lessening to the nor'easter that was ragging outside, but he was afraid for the animals safety and had to make sure that they had food, water, and protection from the elements, or they could freeze to death.

The barn was about a hundred yards from the cabin down a wide path that was lined by trees on both sides. He had told me that they had cleared the path to the barn in this manner, for just this reason, so it would make a safe passage when the weather was severe.

I made some coffee and paced about, too full of nervous energy to sit. I couldn't just stand around watching the clock, and thoughts of breakfast had left my mind the minute Jacob had left the cabin.

I decided to get myself ready in case I had to go out in search of him if he didn't return to the cabin door by exactly 9 o'clock. Running up the stairs, I started rummaging through the drawers in the dresser, in search of the warm clothing I'd need to keep from freezing. I found what I was looking for in the bottom drawer.

Long under ware, thick socks, and a heavy sweater all made of bulky wool. I quickly started changing, taking a quick break to empty my bladder before pulling on the long under ware. It wouldn't be good if I had to pee. I followed these with my jeans, and the sweater that would have kept the Abominable Snowman warm.

I raced back down the stairs, stopping to check the clock which now read 20 minutes after 8, to the Mud Room where I found the heavy boots that I wore when I went to the barn. I pulled them on and laced them up. I checked the heavy coat, and found the fur lined leather gloves tucked in the pocket, and pulled out the smaller pair of snow shoes that I leaned by the door so they would be ready if needed.

Checking the clock again I found that only 30 minutes had passed. I poured myself a cup of coffee hoping it would calm me. I took the first sip and set the cup down just as Bear let out a bark that would have scared the dead.

Jumping up off the couch I watched him as he frantically paced, whining and grumbling deep in his chest, seeming to be looking for a way out. Panic rose in my heart as I said to him, "What is it Boy?"

The dogs erratic behavior made me certain that something was wrong. He had never acted this way in the months I had been here, and I knew I couldn't just sit here doing nothing when every minute might count.

I removed the coffee pot from the stove top and glanced around to make sure nothing could catch fire. I ran to the door, wrapped a heavy wool scarf around my neck and lower face then pulled on the heavy jacket and gloves. Bending over I slipped on the snow shoes and secured them. Once I had the hood up with the strings tightened I was ready.

Calling Bear to me, I grabbed his leash off the hook and tied one end around my waist clipping the other end to the big dog's collar. "Don't go too fast boy or you'll be dragging me on the ground all the way to the barn." He seemed to understand because when I opened the door he gave me enough time to get it closed and latched before moving, instinctively knowing what direction to go.

The wind whipped snow all around me, almost knocking me to the ground as Bear pulled me along the path towards the barn. The blowing snow formed drifts along the right side of the path, but hadn't built up too deep in the middle, making the walk easier than I had anticipated. I could barely make out the trees on either side of the path due to the swirling flakes but with the dogs help we managed to make the trip in record time.

When I got close enough I immediately noticed that the roof on the front of the barn was bare and a large mound of snow it's full length was on the ground. I spotted Griz, his big brown body digging frantically, in an area near the barn's door, knowing instantly that Jacob was buried under that mound.

I grabbed the leash clasp and set Bear free yelling, "Help Griz get him out." Bear ran over, sniffing at the snow, and started digging about 6 feet from where Griz was. Big chunks of snow were flying out behind the dogs as they went to work trying to get to their master. I started digging at the snow between the two dogs with my hands but realized that my fingers would freeze way before I made any progress.

Working my way around the mound, I entered the barn to get the shovel to use to help the dogs dig. I found what I needed and before turning I spotted the sled leaning against the wall. Laying it down I threw the shovel on it and grabbed a pile of horse blankets, adding them to the sled. If Jacob was hurt I'd need this stuff to get him back to the cabin.

Pulling my load I left the cover of the barn. With the mound blocking the wind I was able to get the door closed and secured then headed back to the dogs who were making remarkable progress on the snow pile. I heard Bear let out a bark and ran to him seeing that he had reached Jacobs hands which were covering his face in the small pocket of snow around his head.

The instincts of the dogs amazed me as they teamed up to start clearing the snow from the chest area of where Jacob was laying. I continued to work around his head, exposing his face to the oxygen I knew he needed to survive. His eyelids flickered slightly showing me he was alive. Once his face was cleared I quickly grabbed the shovel and helped the dogs get the heavy snow off him.

When the front of Jacob's jacket was uncovered Bear grabbed it with his strong jaws and pulled, while Griz continued to dig. Between the two dogs it only took a minute or two longer to get his body out. Jacob opened his eyes, looked at me and whispered, "I guess this means breakfast isn't ready," then passed out cold.

Thankfully the sled wasn't too heavy so I picked it up, angling it slightly, and shoved the back end down into a small pile of snow giving me a smooth surface to haul Jacob's body up.

I managed to roll him onto one of the blankets and position him behind the sled. Grabbing the ends of the blanket near his head I pulled hard, making little progress until Bear seemed to figure out my purpose and bit into the blanket hauling Jacob on.

After covering him with the other blankets, I tied one of the leashes to the sled's rope and clipped the other end to Griz's collar. Wrapping the other leash around my waist and to Bear, I grabbed the sled's rope with my hand and was ready to make the trek back to the cabin with my precious cargo.

"Let's go home boys," I ordered the dogs and they moved out, starting slowly and increasing their speed till I was almost running to keep up.

When we arrived at the cabin, the next obstacle was the stairs which turned out to be rather easy when I untied Bear's leash from around my waist and onto the sled. The two dogs pulled it up, through the front door, and over in front of the fireplace with remarkable ease.

Running around gathering blankets and pillows then dumping them on the floor as close to the fire as I dared, I began setting up a makeshift bed on the floor positioning it next to the sled. I didn't have the luxury of actually lifting him onto the real bed like he could do with me. I pulled all the blankets off him and began stripping away all his wet clothing leaving him completely, gloriously naked.

After a quick inspection for possible signs of injury or frostbite, and finding none, I lifted the one side of the sled and rolled him onto the warm dry blankets, his head landing softly on the pile of pillows. It took a little maneuvering but I was able to get him on his back and covered. I sat back on the floor totally exhausted, taking a minute to figure out what I should do next.

Realizing that my own body was chilled, I ran upstairs and stripped off my cold wet clothing. Grabbing the first thing I found, I pulled on one of Jacob's flannel shirts and a pair of warm socks. When I returned to the living room the dogs had curled up on the floor close to their master.

Shoving the sled out of the way I grabbed the last pillows off the couch and the quilt I had brought down from upstairs. Getting as near to Jacob as was possible, without actually laying on top of him, I snuggled up to him and fell asleep instantly, the sound of the Grandfather clock chiming 10.

Jacob

When I woke up, I was on the floor in front of the fireplace with Caitlyn curled up against my side, the two of us buried under a mound of blankets. Looking around I found my dogs close by, both staring at me. When I smiled at them their tails started thumping against the floor, apparently happy I was alive.

I saw the sled by the door and realized that Caitlyn must had gotten me back to the cabin on it. A much easier trip on my body than being dragged back by the dogs. She was amazing; smart, strong, determined, and stubborn as hell, and I loved her with my whole heart. I should have known she wouldn't listen to me, staying in the cabin like I told her to. I'm sure as soon as Bear started up, which I'm sure he did as soon as Griz let out the alert, that she was out the door, snowstorm and all.

Looking down at her nestled against my chest, her right hand over my heart, I could feel the stirring of my body. What was I going to do without her come Spring? Just thinking about her leaving made me ache, and I prayed Winter would last forever. I knew it was an impossibility, but damn, so was time travel.

Caitlyn's cheeks were flushed pink, either from the frigid temperatures earlier, or the heat from the fire, I wasn't sure which, but I had to touch them. As soon as my hand caressed her face her eyes opened. The first words out of her mouth were, "You scared the hell out of me. Don't do that again."

"It wasn't my intent, when I left here, to get buried in snow, Sweetheart," I answered, continuing with, "I was planning on rushing back here and making love to you all afternoon."

"That definitely would have been preferable." "If it wasn't for your dogs, you would be dead Jacob. My God, it was amazing watching them in action, they located you and dug you out. I wouldn't have even known where to start digging."

Hugging her closer I said, "That's why I love their breed so much, they're known for their rescue skills, and have put them to good use over the years." "My first Newfoundland, Old Bear, once saved my mother when she fell through ice. Dad couldn't get to her because the ice was cracking all around her and Old Bear just jumped right in and pulled her out." "Dad gave the dog fresh meat for a week," I finished smiling at the memory.

Rolling up on my chest, Caitlyn looked me in the eye and said, "I'd rather not witness their skills again."

Feeling Caitlyn's loose breasts, covered by just my flannel shirt, made my mind, and my body, instantly switch gears, turning back to my original plan for the day. It took very little urging to get her to go along.

Caitlyn

After a couple of days I was assured that Jacob had no lasting effects from his near death experience. I did, however, insist on accompanying him on his necessary trips to the barn. There was no way I was going to sit in the cabin, all cozy and warm, when I knew there was safety in numbers, besides the only way he could have stopped me from going was to tie me up.

January started out cold and just continued to get colder as the days went by, and into February, forcing us to stay in the cabin and make use of the forms of entertainment we could find inside. We played cards often, me teaching Jacob some of the games that I knew and enjoyed. He always wanted to add stripping as the consequence for a losing hand, and most times this was acceptable to me, as long as there was a roaring fire in the fireplace. My Florida blood was still a lot thinner than his and I didn't think I'd ever be truly warm again.

Near the end of the month I was visited by my friend for the first time since arriving, or as Jacob referred to it, my woman's bleeding. I could tell he was a little disappointed by it's arrival, having hoped I might be pregnant, giving me more reason to stay with him come Spring.

I didn't want to think about leaving Jacob, it hurt too much, and I really didn't believe I could do it. At times I'd think about my family and feel guilty because no matter how much I loved them and missed them I knew, in my heart, I'd miss him more. That guilt kept me from making the final decision.

After a few days of only cuddling we resumed our very active sex life, maybe even more active since the absence, which had definitely made our hearts grow fonder. During a provocative session of strip chess, where I had Jacob down to his underware, I got such a feeling of lust that I attacked him, shoving the chess board and pieces to the floor. I have to admit that cabin fever wasn't a problem that day.

Truthfully it seemed like everything we did during our snow bound confinement ended in sex. I tried teaching Jacob Yoga and after just a few poses we ended up on the rug in front of the fire. Then there was my attempt at teaching him some modern dance moves, which reminded him of his birthday present, and turned into sex on the table. Even making some whipped cream, courtesy of the cows overflowing udders, for our evening's dessert, ended in a rousing sexual experience. We really needed to get out of this cabin, or not.

There was finally a small break in the weather and we ran around outside like two kids, throwing snowballs at each other, the dogs with us enjoying the play. While we were out we made a trip to the barn to take care of the animals for the day, then headed back to the cabin to thaw out in the hot tub, which of course ended in, you guessed it, sex.

The only thing that dampened our idyllic existence was the howling of the wolves at night. When the winds were calm the howls seemed to be extra loud giving me an eerie feeling, almost a foreboding, and I thanked God to be laying in Jacob's loving arms knowing he'd keep me safe. He told me not to worry, that with the dogs in the house, the wolves wouldn't come near, and even if they did they couldn't get in. He also assured me that the barn was secure and that they couldn't get in there either, unless they had learned to use axes.

Before we fell asleep Jacob told me that if the weather held he needed to make a trip to see Samuel in the morning. I didn't like the idea of him going alone and intended to insist that he take both dogs with him. I could be very insistent when I put my mind to it.

Caitlyn

Deciding, since Jacob had to go out for the morning, that I would catch up on some sewing repairs, I gathered up all the items in need of mending and piled them around my favorite spot on the couch. I favored this corner because of it's close proximity to the warm fire. It was friggin freezing out today, and for some reason I was chilled to the bone and couldn't seem to shake it.

Jacob finally agreed to take both Bear and Griz with him when I told him I would be sitting here all morning worried to death about him if he didn't. The sounds of the wolves howling last night had made me wary to the hazards of life in this secluded locale and honestly wanted him to take the dogs to keep him safe while he was out alone in the wilderness. Jacob had only agreed with my solemn promise not to leave the cabin. He needn't have worried about that, I had no intentions of stepping one foot outside in the bitter cold today.

I was dressed in my jeans and a long sleeved sweater, even wearing my boots with heavy socks, to keep my feet warm. I popped my ear buds in my ears and was enjoying my music, to help make this boring sewing task a little more enjoyable. I was totally oblivious to everything, but the song playing and the garment in my hand, when I became suddenly aware of a presence in the cabin.

I smelled the foul stench before I even saw him. Looking up I was surprised by the hulking male figure standing on the other side of the room, malevolence radiating from him. He must have come in through the mud room, and without Bear to alert me, was now glaring at me with loathing in his eyes.

Reaching up slowly, I pulled on the ear bud wire, removing them and letting them fall to the couch, restoring my sense of hearing just in time to hear his one word command, "Food!"

Not moving I pointed towards the kitchen.

My actions seemed to infuriate him as he bellowed, "Get me some damn food, woman."

Rising from the couch quickly, I rushed to the kitchen, my mind visualizing the knives kept there. He seemed to sense what I was thinking and taunted, "I'll snap you like a twig if you try anything, bitch."

While I was pulling out food and putting it on the table, I was sizing him up. He was as tall as Jacob but probably outweighed him by a good 50 pounds, and with his heavy coat he appeared massive. His dirt caked hair, hung to his shoulders, giving me the impression of a feral animal. I tried to avoid looking at his eyes because his angry stare caused my fear level to escalate, clouding my judgment. I needed to keep a clear head.

After about 20 minutes he stopped eating and let out a disgusting belch. God, he made my skin crawl. His attention on me now, I could see his thoughts had changed from food to something I didn't even want to think about. Instinctively I backed up, causing him to sneer as he said, "There's no place for you to go little lady, why don't you just come over here and make it easy on yourself."

The words "No Way In Hell" screamed in my head as I looked around for a way out.

He got up, ready to pursue, when the sounds of barking warned him of someone's impending arrival. The dog's furious attempts to scratch through the door with their large paws caused my attention to be diverted just long enough for him to grab me. Jerking me up against his chest, he hauled me backwards towards the kitchen, where he grabbed my biggest, sharpest knife, and pressed it firmly against my throat. This is the scene Jacob came into when he burst through the door, rifle in hand.

Jacob

My face was nearly frozen by the time I made it to Samuel's cabin. The February cold didn't seem to effect the dog's who were still romping around, and delighted to see Isaac's two big Bloodhounds. Knocking, and entering at the same time, I found Hattie Mae, a worried expression on her face, talking to Samuel and Isaac.

Isaac had just gotten back from town and was warning them that William Kelly had escaped from jail and was last seen heading towards our part of the mountains. Kelly was a brutal murderer, who'd finally been captured after months of vigilant searching by state lawmen, and had been in the local jail waiting to be escorted to the state prison. It'd taken dozens of men to track him down, and now he was on the loose again.

Isaac was saying, "I was real glad I had brought the bloods with me, or I woulda been jumpin at every little thing all the way back home," when my thoughts of Caitlyn, alone in the cabin, sent fear tearing through me.

Running from the cabin, I rushed back to my horse, mounted, and whistling for the dogs, took off like a bat out of hell, thankful that I had taken it easy on Champ on the way over here. The dog's sensing my urgency, kept up the hurried pace, staying just ahead, directing me with their movements towards the quickest path.

During the ride my mind kept going over, and over, why I had been so stupid to leave her alone. "What the hell was wrong with me?" I thought, against my every instinct, I had let her talk me into taking Bear with me, when I always left him there for her protection. If anything happened to her I'd never forgive myself.

I made it back to the cabin swiftly. As I got close, the dogs sensed something was wrong, and running ahead, were now barking, clawing, and biting at the door trying to get in. Their actions making me apprehensive, I readied my rifle, and headed for the door.

Crashing through without warning, I came face to face with my greatest fear. Kelly had Caitlyn, her body plastered in front of him as a shield, a large knife pressing against her throat. The dogs went wild, aggressively trying to get to him around her.

Kelly bellowed, "Call off the dogs or I'll slice her head right off."

Knowing he meant it, I did as he bid, and ordered the dogs to heel, watching as they immediately moved back and sat, flanking my sides, their watchful stares fixed on Kelly.

Keeping my eyes glued on him, I could see Caitlyn staring intently at me, but not meeting my eyes. Her look pensive, not so much from fear, but determination. I didn't know what she was thinking, but I knew that calculating look of hers.

"Drop your rifle," Kelly barked out, pressing the knife tighter against Caitlyn's throat causing her slight whimper.

Holding my rifle out to the side, I spoke, my voice confirming my raging state of mind as I growled out, "Let her go Kelly, you'll never get out of here alive if you hurt her, and by God if you do, by the time I'm finished with your sorry ass, you'll be begging me to put you out of your misery."

Kelly's eyes were darting back and forth, my words causing him to falter slightly, loosening his hold just enough to set Caitlyn into motion.

I watched, with amazement, as she lifted her left leg and stomped down on the top of Kelly's foot with her boot heal, and at the same time punch back with her right fist using every ounce of strength she had and catching him square in the crotch. The knife clattered to the ground as Kelly sunk to his knees, but instead of running away from him, Caitlyn spun around and with a loud "Yaaa,." placed a well-aimed, booted side kick right to the center of his face, crushing his nose and sending him flying backwards, slamming his head into the stone floor. The dogs jumped into action, quickly taking up their posts, guarding the unconscious prisoner.

I was so dumbfounded by what I had just witnessed that for a moment I just stood there, staring at Kelly's prone form. Finally looking at Caitlyn's face, I saw her tear filled eyes, and walked to her with open arms. When she was safely wrapped in my embrace I heard her sob against my chest, "That Son-of-a-bitch ate the rest of our pie."

Holding her till she calmed, I finally asked, "Where'd you learn to do that?"

"Having two daughters, my father insisted on years of self defense classes," she answered. "I'm really glad to see he didn't waste his money," she finished.

"I'm sure glad I didn't try any of the things that I had wanted to do to you when we first met," I said, grateful that she was okay. "And one more thing Caitlyn, if you ever want me to save you some pie, please just let me know." This finally brought a small chuckle from her, as we heard a commotion outside.

Samuel, Hattie and Isaac arrived, running in with looks of fear, and concern, on their faces, that quickly changed to guffaws of laughter, when they learned that William Kelly had been brought down by a 120 pound woman.

The men tied Kelly up securely, threw him in the back of the sled, and hauled his unconscious body back to the jail in town.

Hattie Mae stayed with Caitlyn, securely locked inside, with Bear on guard. They spent a couple of hours enjoying each other's company, and baking another pie.

Caitlyn

For the rest of the month of February and into the first week of March, Jacob wouldn't let me out of his sight, even insisting I accompany him again on his daily trips to the barn. Since the incident with Kelly, Jacob's protective instincts had kicked in big time, constantly keeping me within eyesight. It seemed like every time I turned around he was bumping into my ass, and I didn't mean in a good way. He was driving me crazy.

No matter how much you love someone, being around them 24/7 was just too damned much togetherness, and I finally blew up. "Jacob please, give me some breathing room for God's sake," I yelled at him after walking into his chest and dropping all the vegetables I was carrying for our dinner meal.

His hurt expression made me instantly sorry for my outburst as I watched him slam out the back door to the freezing porch, without even taking his jacket. After about 15 minutes, my guilt sent me out after him. He was just standing there against the railing, staring off towards the snow covered mountains.

I wasn't sure if he had heard me come out, but when I called his name he turned to me. Walking to him, I gripped his rib cage with my hands, and bowed my head into his chest, hearing his heartbeat. "I'm sorry Jacob," I said, meaning it.

He reached down and lifted my chin with his icy fingers, and kissed my lips with his blue tinged ones. Convincing him to come back inside, I led him to the couch, even giving up my warm corner to him. We didn't say anything for a long time, just sat together, close enough that our shadow, cast on the wall by the flames in the fireplace, looked like one.

His soft words of apology finally breaking the silence as he said, "I'm sorry too, Caitlyn, but the thought of you getting hurt because of my lack of common sense makes me feel like a complete idiot. Thank God your smart enough for the both of us."

"Excuse me Jacob, but I could never fall in love with a stupid man," I told him, continuing, "Remember it was my idea for you to take both dogs that day."

"It never should have happened, and Bear would've never let that scum in the cabin if he'd been here, like he should have been. I've lived here all my life and I know the dangers of living in this secluded place, yet I left you alone. What does that say about me?"

"Jacob bad things, and bad people, happen all over the world, not just here, and if we live our whole life with the fear of something bad happening, it will kill us both." Going on, I explained, "You do what you can to be prepared for the obstacles life throws at you, so I think it's about time for you to teach me how to use that rifle of yours."

This idea seemed to spark his interest, and he asked, "You've never shot a gun?" With my negative nod, he asked, "How about a bow and arrow?"

"No to that, too," I answered, telling him, "The only weapons I've ever used are nunchucks, sais, and a bostaff, all from Karate lessons. I could probably teach you a thing or two about stick fighting, if you'd like."

"Alright, he said, laughing at my suggestion, I'll teach you to shoot guns, and arrows, and you can show me how to fight with little sticks."

"Don't you laugh at me, Mister," I warned him, heading for my broom to demonstrate a few moves. Snatching it up, I moved back across the room towards him, flipping it, cracking it on the floor, and slicing it through the air as I went. Throwing in a few, "Yaa's," to punctuate certain movements, my last, stopping right next to the side of his head just before making contact, my narrowed eyes staring right into his. The exertion to my unused muscles filling me with exhilaration.

"Damn, you look sexy right now, my little warrior princess," he told me, making me burst out laughing. "I guess you could teach me a few things about stick fighting," he admitted.

"Right now I need to get back to cooking since I know the only thing you can do in the kitchen is make eggs," I told him, heading back to our dinner.

"That's not the only thing I can do in the kitchen Sweetheart," he said heading in my direction, and then demonstrating his skills when he got to me.

Oh well, I guess we were going to be having a late dinner this night.

Jacob

The next morning I went to the barn alone, leaving Caitlyn in the cabin by herself, with Bear on guard, of course. The first thing I did there was find a hard piece of wood, about 5 ½ feet long. Using my low angle plane I shaved off enough wood to leave a rounded stick about half again as thick as a broom handle.

I worked on it for about an hour making sure it was sanded smooth and slid through my hands without the chance of splinters, leaving the ends smooth but blunt. Swinging it around a few times I could see how something like this, in the hands of someone who knew how to use it, could do a lot of damage to an adversary.

After taking care of the animal's needs, I headed up to the loft area and dug out the bow and arrows, and the target that I had used for practice when I was learning. I found my mother's bow which was a little smaller than mine, and checked the strings on both, finding them in good working order.

Checking the arrows I found that the shafts were straight with the attached fletching in suitable shape, and the arrowheads nice and sharp. I was looking forward to teaching Caitlyn how to shoot, knowing with her aim she would pick it up quickly.

Finishing up in the barn, I grabbed the homemade bostaff and headed back to the cabin, twirling it as I walked. Truthfully I was also looking forward to Caitlyn showing me some of her moves from the night before. She had been very impressive, and deadly, with her little broom stick. I couldn't wait to see her with this in her hands.

Walking in the door of the cabin, I was greeted by the back of her swaying body. I knew she was listening to her I-pod and hadn't heard me come in as she continued her silent dance while dusting the mantle.

Standing across the room from her, I could actually follow the beat of the song she was listening to as I watched her rhythmic movements, abandoning herself to her music. She must have sensed my presence because she turned around and looked at me, inviting me to join her with just the look in her eyes, that is, until she saw the stick in my hand.

She pulled the ear buds out of her ears as she headed straight towards me, a big smile on her face. "Where'd you get that?" she asked, as her hand grasped at the handmade Bo staff.

"I made it for you," I told her, handing it to her and watching as she twirled it in a figure 8 motion, back and forth in front of her body. She seemed thrilled with my gift.

"Wow, it's perfect. Much better than my broom."

"I'm glad you like it. I wasn't sure how long to make it, so I had to guess at the proper length, but I thought about your height would be a good start," I said, watching her enthusiastic reaction.

"This is great Jacob, nice weight too, as good as the real thing. Thank you"

"Your welcome, and while I was in the barn I pulled out the Archery equipment. If you feel like it, we can go down after lunch for your first lesson," I suggested.

"Sounds like a plan to me, but no stripping if I miss the target. The barns too cold for Strip Archery," I informed him with a sly smile.

"Your taking all the fun out of it," I told her, then finished with, "I'm sure I can find a number of ways to warm you up if you prove to be a poor archer."

With a quick little snap to my bicep with her new stick, she headed to the kitchen to see to lunch.

Caitlyn

After a quick lunch of chicken noodle soup, Jacob and I walked to the barn to begin my Archery lessons. I brought along my new stick and enjoyed twirling it around as we walked. When we got there I immediately went to Starlight and gave her the carrot I had brought for her, not forgetting Champ, and the two stock horses, that had no names. I suggested Buck and Kick, seeing as they didn't have the best dispositions and tried to keep you at leg's length with both these maneuvers.

Jacob set the target up at one end of the barn, away from all the animals, to insure their safety, and then started to give me verbal instructions on the proper use of the bow. After way too much explaining, I asked him to just give me a demonstration.

Standing perpendicular to the target, he held up the bow, hooked the end with the feathers on the string, and pulled back. I have to admit he looked very masculine, and quite hot. When he released the arrow it flew straight at the target hitting just outside the bull's eye. I thought this was an excellent first shot, he complained, mentioning that it had been a long time since he'd used his bow.

After shooting all six arrows he had four in the bull's eye and one more just outside the line. It was my turn to try. I copied his stance and pulled back on the smaller bow, the way he instructed. My arrow slipped just as I released it and it went flying into the loft area, luckily missing the chickens who were roosting up there. Jacob had to rethink that whole animal safety thing, and I noticed even he moved farther behind me for my second attempt.

My next shot was slightly better, it still missed the target completely, but at least it stayed on the bottom floor of the barn. Archery was a lot harder than it looked, and my next three arrows still didn't hit the mark. Finally my last arrow, with extensive aiming, actually hit the outside edge of the target, and stuck. I was ecstatic with my success, but Jacob just rolled his eyes.

We shot two more sets of six arrows, Jacob's second set all hit the bull's eye, mine didn't do as well, but I did improve, hitting the outer edges of the target with two. Our third set was similar, Jacob, showing off again, hitting the bull's eye with all his arrows.

I was pleased when the first of my six arrows hit the outside of the biggest color ring. I got so excited that I swung around with my next arrow in the bow and almost caught Jacob in the chest with it. The next four I shot, flew closer, but didn't actually hit the target, and my last arrow stuck into the barn wall.

At the end of the third set, Jacob announced, chuckling, "I've risked my life enough for one day," putting an end to my first lesson. Hey, I didn't think my effort was that bad for my first attempt, but I was glad that Jacob didn't push the stripping thing because I would have been bare assed naked after the second set.

After putting away all the archery equipment, I gave Jacob a little demonstration with the bostaff, having lots of room to let loose in the open barn. Performing the kata that I had used when I earned my black belt, I put on quite a show for my one person audience. A couple of times I intentionally made aggressive moves in his direction, seeing his eyes widen with surprise. My main reason for this forceful display was to make him think twice about commenting on my archery skills.

When I was finished, I did a little bow, and then asked, "What do you think?"

"I think maybe I shouldn't mess with you when you have your stick in your hands," he answered, then said, starting to laugh, "I also think I should stand as far away from you as I possibly can when your shooting arrows."

I couldn't help joining him in his laughter.

On the way back to the cabin, Jacob told me he would like to learn the Karate moves, even if it was just for the exercise. My mind instantly imagined him, shirtless, his muscles flexing as he stretched in the kata movements. When he caught me looking at him, he asked, "What are you thinking about Caitlyn? You've got an intriguing look in your eyes."

"I was just thinking that you better get your own stick, because I'm not sharing mine with you."

Raising his eyebrows he said, "That's a little selfish Love, I'd be happy to share my stick with you."

With a quick maneuver I spun around intent on giving him a little tap, but he anticipated my move and caught my stick in his hand, giving it a tug. He thought he had me, but knowing I could never get it out of his grasp, I just let go and took off running in the direction of the cabin, leaving him standing there with my stick in his hand.

I was almost to the cabin by the time he caught up to me. Dropping my stick he grabbed me and spun me around a couple of times before letting me down, both of us laughing like children.

When we were finished playing we went inside, all the annoyances from the past couple of weeks, due to our forced confinement in this isolated place, wiped out by our contentment. I loved this man, and if I had to be stuck alone with someone, I couldn't think of anyone I'd rather be with than him.

Kathryn's Journals

"Enlightenment from the past can lend a hand to elucidate the future"

Jacob

This Winter has been one of the coldest I can remember, that is on the outside of the cabin, inside it has been the warmest. From the wind's fierce gales, of the coldest artic air so far, I could tell that March was definitely coming in like a lion.

Knowing how rough the harsh climate was on Caitlyn, I made the decision to let her read my mother's journals. Up till this point I was afraid that reading them would probably scare the hell out of her as to what life was like, year after year, in this remote location.

My mother's words had a way of making you feel every experience she had endured, especially her feelings of isolation, and loneliness, during her first years here. I also recall that as time went by she had found true happiness in her home here with my father, and I really wanted Caitlyn to read about that.

I went up to the closet in our room and just as I was pushing the clothes back out of the way she popped up behind me, asking, "What are you doing?"

"I have something that I thought you might find interesting," I told her, as, bending down, I stuck my finger in the knot hole and pulled the panel off the hiding place, her looking over my shoulder the whole time. Inside was the six journals all wrapped in oilcloth to protect them.

"What are those?" she asked, her curiosity peaked.

"They're my mother's journals," I said, adding, "She started writing them when she first moved here with my father in 1848 right after they got married."

Caitlyn's excitement evident in her face as I handed her the first volume and grabbed the other five to carry downstairs. When we got to the living room Caitlyn quickly sat in her corner of the couch and opened the wrapping on the first journal. She ran her hand over the leather cover and opened the flap, reading the first written words; *Personal Journal of Kathryn Marie "Kat" Wilkinson,* and the date, *November 1848.*

I sat down next to her and admitted, "I wasn't going to let you read them because I was afraid that some of her words might influence your decision whether you should stay, but then I realized that everything she writes is not gloomy. My mother was honestly happy here with my father and she conveys that with her words too."

Caitlyn looked into my eyes and reaching up touched my face, saying, "Thank you for sharing these with me."

"I also thought it would be a good way for you to get to know them both. They were wonderful, passionate people who I miss every day. I wish you could have met them, I know they would have loved you." She leaned in and gave me a tender kiss, confirming that my choice had been the right one.

Caitlyn

Turning to the first entry I began reading and let myself reside in Kathryn's life through her words.

November 8, 1848
My new life's adventure began when I married the true love of my life, Jacob James Wilkinson, on November 6, 1848 in a simple civil service in Boston, Massachusetts. After living in this bustling city all my life with my older sister, Anna who I adored, and my loving parents, I was now embarking on a journey to a small farm in the North Country of New York with my husband of 2 days.

I met my Jake 2 months after my 18th birthday and fell so in love with him I would have traveled to Timbuktu to be with him. During our 8 months courtship he shared with me his dreams of a farm in the foothills of the Adirondack Mountains near the border of Canada.

Jake had described the beauty of the area he had visited many times over the years, the mountain vistas ever changing with the seasons. I could see that his passion for this life was deep-rooted, but his passion for me was even stronger, which he proved when he asked me to be his wife and told me he would give it all up if I didn't want to leave my family. He said he would be happy anywhere as long as I was in his life.

I remember the kiss we shared, and telling him that I would be honored to help him make his dreams come true. So that's where we were now, on a train headed for Clinton County, New York. My mother's words echoed in my mind, "When you find your true love, it doesn't matter where you are because 'you' are home for each other." I planned to make Jake happy and give him the home he dreamed of.

November 9, 1848
We've arrived in the little town of Clinton, if you can really call the couple of wood buildings a town. Jake had all preparation made ahead of time and we were met by his friend, Charlie, with the horses and wagon, loaded up our trunks, and then headed to the General Store for the supplies we would need. By the time we were finished the wagon was loaded down with what looked like enough supplies for a year.

Jake said he had one more stop to make, and after about a half hours ride through some of the most beautiful country imaginable, we stopped at an old barn and were greeted by an elderly couple. Before he could even introduce us, out bounded two of the biggest, most boisterous, dogs I'd ever seen in my life.

The larger of the two was pure black, almost a midnight blue when the sun hit it's coat. The other one also had long black fur, but it was broken up by a white patch on it's chest. Jake jumped out of the wagon jostling around with the two monsters while I stayed safely in the wagon. When he looked at me with his big boyish grin, showing off his dimples, I couldn't help but smile back. He was the most handsome man.

Our little wagon train continued up into the hills, Charlie following along on horseback to help Jake unload. Thank God for that because I was exhausted and fell asleep against my husband's chest, rocked by the swaying wagon on the way to the cabin.

When we finally came out in a small clearing, I got my first look at what was going to be my new home. The cabin was small but in pretty decent shape. The barn next to it was a completely different story, appearing to be better suited for fire wood, than shelter for the horses.

I have to admit that the mountain backdrop was gorgeous, with shades of crimson, amber, and gold on full display. The beauty of the land was undeniable. The Autumn air was crisp and cool, and so clean compared to the city that you could feel it's purity in your lungs. I could see why Jake was so enamored of this part of the country.

With Charlie's help they unloaded the wagon and now it's time for me to get to work.

There was no entries for the next four days. I figured Kathryn was probably really busy trying to set up her new home and get settled in during this period. When I started reading the next one I realized that she was coping with a lot more than just moving.

November 14, 1848
The winds of the storm that blew in last night cut through me like a knife, chilling me to the bone. The only warmth I can find in my new isolated world, is in my husbands arms, but he's so busy getting the farm ready for the coming Winter that I'm left alone most of the day, with only a monstrous, slobbering dog to keep me company.

I have gotten the cabin in some semblance of order, and if it wasn't so cold inside, I might even consider it homey. I've figured out how to use the old wood stove and have gotten some pleasure out of cooking for Jake. He really loves to eat, which makes me eager to please. Thank you Mother for teaching me this enjoyable, and useful skill. I think we both would have starved to death if you hadn't. I miss you Mommy, Daddy, and Anna very much.

There was another break in Kathryn's entries, this time a whole week passed before she wrote again. Her last entry made me realize that she really hadn't been prepared for the changes her life was going through. At 18 years old, who could expect her to, she was still a girl.

November 21, 1848
The storm that started a week ago lasted 4 days and brought a couple of feet of slushy snow that added to the misery of going outside the cabin to do anything. I can't believe I've only been here 2 weeks, it already feels like an eternity since I've seen Anna and my parents. I miss them terribly, and weep with my loneliness when Jakes not home. So far I've managed to hide my feelings because I don't want to spoil his jubilation, he loves it here.

When Jake holds me in his arms at night I feel like I could go through anything, as long as I have him to comfort me. He is my home now, and wherever he goes, I'll follow.

Kathryn's entries dwindled over the next couple of months, with only a date and a couple of words that confirmed her life was not improving, actually is was becoming more desolate. On Christmas Day, her first with Jake, all she had written was "Merry Christmas." Her world had crumbled and I flipped through the next couple of pages looking for a sign that she was alright. This is what I found instead.

January 31, 1849
Seeing my world through naïve eyes, I now realize that I was not prepared for what life had in store for me. It wasn't the wonderful adventure that I had expected, instead a fight for survival. Can I persevere?

February 11, 1849
My loneliness, and fear, is magnified by the soulful howling of the wolves. Jacob's companionship my only solace in this bleak existence.

February 27, 1849
The cold seeps into my veins turning my blood to icy sludge, making me believe that when it reaches my heart, it will just freeze. I have no tears left to cry. I know Jake is aware of what's happening to me, I can see it in his eyes, looking at me with sorrow when I turn away from him. I'm ruining his happiness, his dream. Doesn't he know I need his warmth to bring me back. Please Jake, help me.

I slid the ribbon marker in the journal and set it down, my unfettered tears streaming down my cheeks. My heart went out to Kathryn, her beautiful young spirit being crushed with the isolation of her new life.

When I looked up I found Jacob's eyes on me, and I heard him say what I was feeling, "The first few pages are really hard to read. My father loved my mother wholeheartedly, it would have destroyed him if anything had happened to her."

Moving across the room, he sat next to me and continued, "They were stuck here, alone, he had no way to get her out until the weather cleared, and from what he told me, that was his plan as soon as possible. He felt he had to get my mother away from here, or she would die, and it would be his fault."

"Your mother was so young and innocent. She had no idea what to expect when she left her family to come here," I said, still feeling her despair. "I need to stop reading for a while, I'll fix us dinner. You are hungry aren't you?"

With Jacob's nod, I got up and headed for the kitchen. He followed me there and wrapped me in his arms, nuzzling the back of my neck, while telling me, "You know she was alright, they were together for 32 years, remember she wrote five more journals after that one."

His words and embrace cheered me up. We spent a quiet evening together then went up to bed. Jacob's tender lovemaking that night removed all thoughts of his mother's words and brought me to the here and now, with him. Falling asleep against his chest, I knew I'd always be safe in his arms.

Waking up early the next morning, I threw together a hasty breakfast, anxious to get back to the journal. The winds had died down outside and Jacob told me he had some work to do in the barn, heading off with Griz after a quick kiss.

I grabbed another cup of coffee and moved to my couch corner, picking up the journal and turning to the page where I had left off. Kathryn's next entry gave me a little hope that her spirit wasn't completely broken.

March 11, 1849
Today I forced myself to get out of the fetal position I've grown fond of. The cold has abated slightly and made way for a few rays of sunlight to actually shine down from the heavens. Maybe God is still watching.

March 15, 1849
Charlie came by to see Jake today. When he looked at me I saw his eyes dart to Jake with concern. I was a mess, an embarrassment to my husband that caused my shame. When my tears returned after a two week absence Jake held me in his arms and asked me why. All I could say was, I'm sorry.

April 3, 1849
The snow is starting to melt, I can see the tiniest specks of green starting to peak out of the frozen earth, reaching for the warmth of the sun. I want it too, the warmth, to bring a thawing to my heart. I want to breath again, and feel. I want my husband back.

April 11, 1849
The rain started while we were outside, Jake put his arm around my waist and we ran together to get inside before the drenching downpour soaked us to the skin. My laughter at our childish race causing a look of joy to return to Jake's eyes. I had to reach up and caress his cheek, his dimple under my thumb. That one simple gesture brought him into my arms again. His love bringing me back to life.

When the storm passed we stepped outside arm in arm and saw the rainbow over the mountains, it's brilliance like a sign from the Lord that all was right again in our world.

I sat there on the couch weeping with my happiness for these two lost souls, who found each other again. I thought about Jacob. He'd shown me in so many ways that I was the reason for his new found happiness. If I left in the Spring to return to my family would I ever be able to come back to him? Could I live the rest of my life without him? The word "no" invaded my mind as I turned back to the journal.

April 18, 1849
Jake and I stood on the new porch he had added to the cabin, looking up at the full moon illuminating the outline of the mountains with an alluring glow. The darkness of the sky a backdrop for the millions of glimmering stars. It was the most beautiful night sky I'd ever seen, dark and bright at the same time.

Jake told me we could leave in about a week, that the snow in the pass was melting. I was taken-aback by his declaration since we hadn't broached this subject as of yet. When I told him I'd like to stay another month, and thinking to myself, "before shattering your dreams," he told me that whatever I decided was best for me, was fine with him. I feel so blessed to have found this compassionate man to share my life with.

I devoured the next six months of Kathryn's journal, delighting in the happiness of the young couple who had decided to stay in their mountain home. By October I noticed a little trepidation creeping back into her writings with the coming of Winter. Her fear of loosing herself again in the gloom, starting to resurface.

October 25, 1849
The temperatures are dropping, bringing back the bitter nights, and my dread. Jake has let his beard grow as an added source of warmth for his face, but in doing so has hidden his smiling dimples which are a source of warmth for my heart. I know he'd remove it if I asked, but I have to consider his comfort when he's out in the frigid air. He's still so handsome, in a mountain man kind of way.

November 27, 1849
The first storm blew in last night turning our warm home into a frozen box. Jake kept the fire in the fireplace burning high to try to chase away the deadly chill I was feeling. He also manages to warm my soul in our bed each night. I have to stay strong for him, and for me. I can't let the iciness take over again.

December 1, 1849
My constant companion on these endless days has the biggest, most adoring, brown eyes. I never imagined I could love this oversized canine the way I do. She stays by my side no matter what my activities entail for the day. I've changed her name to Snowflake because the fluffy white markings on her chest remind me of one, besides I didn't feel that Blackie was an acceptable name for my dearly loved friend. She seems to like the change and won't respond anymore when called by her old title, which seems to irritate Jake a bit. I find it quite humorous.

December 14, 1849
As cold as I feel, I'm still lucid. I'm looking forward to Christmas with my husband this year, which shows improvement of my mind-set compared with last year. When Charlie was here last week I asked him to get me a couple of tins of the mints Jakes like to keep at our bedside. Jake doesn't think I know what he's up to but whenever I smell the peppermint on his breath it usually means I'll be a happy woman.

December 20, 1849
I've notice Jakes increased attentiveness. At times this is reassuring, at other times it's annoying and I want to tell him to just leave me alone, but I don't. I never want him to leave me alone.

December 26, 1849
Jake and I had a truly romantic Christmas. I refuse to expound on the details, but it was a day, and night, I'll remember always. I love you Jacob James Wilkinson, with my soul.
P.S. He loved the mints

January 5, 1850
A couple of days ago Jake and I were surprised by the arrival of Samuel, Hattie Mae and their two sons, Isaac and Henry. They were en-route to Canada, running away from a Slave Master down south. Poor little Isaac was so sick that I don't believe he would have survived without our help. Jake brought the terrified family to the cabin where I tended to their sick child, and made sure they were all fed. I'll never forget the desperation in Hattie Mae's eyes when she looked at me, pleading for help for her son.

The next day Isaac was much improved. His parent's fear of capture resulted in them wanting to continue their journey. With the weather condition declining I asked Jake to let them stay, telling him that maybe they could help us while we helped them. Honestly, I don't give a damn what color their skin is, they're human beings with hearts and souls, and I need them, probably more than they need us. I believe he was considering my loneliness of last year when he agreed.

Accepting our offer, the William's family moved into the warmest part of the barn. Jake helped Samuel make it as comfortable as possible for them. While they worked together, Jake found that Samuel was very knowledgeable about farming, and the two talked about Jake's plans for the coming Spring.

Hattie Mae spent a lot of time with me during the first few days buoying my spirits ten-fold. Her beautiful brown face and kind eyes were reassuring, and her laughter, when I finally heard it, delighted me. I couldn't have asked for a better friend to keep me from turning in on myself again. Thank you God for sending them to us. I'm sure their companionship will take away some of the bleakness of Winter in these mountains.

The rest of Kathryn's January entries told of the bond that was forming between these two lonely young families. Their struggle for survival in this harsh environment, cemented their friendship as no other way could have. It made me happy knowing that their bond had lasted for so many years.

Hearing the clock bong in 12:00 noon, I put the journal away and headed for the kitchen knowing Jacob would be home soon for lunch. He walked in about ten minutes later, and after giving me a kiss, stated, "You must have been reading all morning."

"What makes you think that?" I asked, continuing our lunch prep.

"I don't smell anything delicious baking," he answered, looking in the cookie jar for a little treat before lunch. Grabbing the last cookie, he popped the whole thing in his mouth.

"I think I remember you accusing me of trying to make you fat," I mentioned as I sliced some of the left-over chicken. "I wouldn't want to be responsible for ruining that fine body of yours sir," I finished, giving him the once over with my eyes.

"Your so cute when your trying to sucker me in, woman."

"Hmmm . . . sucker me in, that's an interesting phrase," I said giving him a wicked look, my eyes lingering on the crotch area of his pants.

"Caitlyn, you better stop now or your afternoon is going to be unavailable for reading," he informed me with a rakish smile.

Setting down the knife and washing my hands, I walked to him, and standing on tip toes leaned into the full length of his body for a lingering kiss, murmuring into his mouth, "I'll race you upstairs."

He scooped me up in his arms and headed for the stairs, saying, "You can save your energy for other things my Love."

When we returned downstairs about an hour later we were both starving. I finished preparing what I had started earlier and we sat together enjoying our afternoon meal.

Stuffing the last bite in his mouth, chewing and swallowing quickly, he asked, "Do you need a chicken for dinner?"

"Are you already thinking about your next meal sir?" I asked incredulously.

"After the appetizer you served with lunch, how can I think about anything else?"

"Point taken," I said, smiling at him, then added, "As for your chicken question, no, we're going to finish up the stew. The chickens can have a reprieve for one more day."

"Any chance you can pull yourself away from reading long enough to throw in some biscuits?" he asked, that grin of his returning.

"I'll see if I have the time," I answered drolly, bending over his back and giving him a smooch on the cheek as I grabbed the dishes off the table.

He got up, and giving me a pat on the rear, headed for the door, calling out, "I'll see you later Love."

I rushed through the clean up and took enough time to pull out a few ingredients to make him a sweet surprise for dessert, then headed back to my spot on the couch, anxious to continue my reading. I don't think I ever enjoyed a book as much as I was enjoying this one.

Finding my page, I pored over the entries, devouring each word Kathryn wrote. Her strength and endurance through the winter months made possible by her new found friendship with Hattie. And watching

Hattie's young boys playing around the cabin started a yearning in her for the children she hoped to have with Jake.

By Spring 1850 all their work loads multiplied. Kat and Hattie planted a large vegetable garden, which they tended daily, and tried to do as much work around the farm as they could to free up their husbands who, besides running the farm, were also building a cabin for the William's family. Kat, and Jake, couldn't stand the idea of them spending another cold Winter in the barn.

The farm was thriving. Samuel's knowledge of planting and harvesting increased their production and Jake had to hire workers to help with the abundant crops. He also utilized them to help with the cabin building, including some additions to their own, and renovations on the barn. By the end of the Summer Jake was able to purchase another 300 acres and during the Autumn he and Samuel planned out the planting for the following Spring.

By the end of December, just before Christmas, Hattie Mae and Samuel moved into their new home. They were still neighbors, Kat had insisted on it, the two cabins separated by a couple of acres of land, with the barn between them. They spent the holiday together like one big happy family.

Kathryn's postings for '51' were about everyday life on the farm, with the only big change from their daily routines being, the ground clearing for the new cabin Jake was going to build for his wife. He had picked a location partway up the mountain with views from all sides that Jake said, "almost matched the beauty of his wife."

Another thing that happened in the late Spring of '51' was that Snowflake had her first litter of pups, 8 in all, 3 females and 5 males. Jake had bred her with a beautiful copper male from Harland and Molly's farm and the puppies were a beautiful mix of colors. Jake and Kat kept the all brown male, and Hattie and Samuel took a brown/black mixed female.

The Winter of '52' was brutal. The temp dropping below 0 for the whole month of January and half of February. By the time their world thawed out, the end of April, Kat realized she was pregnant. All the sharing of body heat to keep each other warm had done the trick.

April 26, 1852
Waking up this morning, I was assailed by a bout of nausea so intense I thought I would eject my entire stomach along with it's contents. Thank God Jake had left early and wasn't witness to my repugnant display. Thinking I was dying, I dragged myself out the door and across to Hattie. When I told her of my condition, she chuckled at me.

At first I was taken aback by her lack of sympathy and concern for my well being, and then she asked when my last woman's bleeding was. Thinking back, I finally remembered it had been in January. Joy filled me and I shared it with Hattie by squeezing her in a close hug, which ended abruptly when a second bout of dry heaves racked my body, and doubled me over.

Hattie took me in to her home and fixed me a wonderful cup of tea with honey, and a slice of dry toast, telling me to eat it in small bites followed by little sips. By the time I was finished I almost felt like myself again. Before going back to my own cabin I made her promise not to tell Samuel about the baby. I wanted to tell Jake first. She assured me she could keep her mouth shut, which actually caused me to erupt into tear inducing hysteria, knowing how she loved to talk.

By the time Jake came home this evening I was ready to burst with the excitement of my news. Jake, noticing my cheerful mood, embraced me in a loving hug. Unfortunately his odorous body from working outside in the heat all day brought on the nausea again, and before I could say anything I was running for a bucket. Between my fits of retching I managed to inform him that he was going to be a father.

It hadn't been the beautiful scene I had imagined, but when the nausea passed, we laughed, and cried together, with our shared joy.

Hearing the clock gong 3:00. I closed the journal and jumped up from the couch, heading to the kitchen. I didn't want Jacob to come home and catch me still sitting with my eyes glued to the book. The last entry had me in a cheerful mood the rest of the afternoon. It had been so enjoyable, and funny, causing the big smile that was still on my face when he walked in.

"What has you all smiles?" he asked, kissing my cheek and looking around trying to see what I was baking.

"Kat just told Jake that she's pregnant, and the poor dear is so sick," I said giggling.

Remembering the entry himself, Jacob smiled, then said, "I love the way you talk about them like they're friends of yours, these are my parents, remember, and by the way Caitlyn, women in 1883 do not use the word pregnant."

Bowing my head in a submissive gesture, I said, "Please accept my apology for the impropriety of my words kind Sir," and then pulled the chocolate chip pound cake out of the oven, setting it right in front of him on the counter.

His burst of laughter at my subservient sham was quickly followed by, "Mmmm, that smells good."

I think it really is true, that the way to a man's heart is through his stomach.

Jacob

Winter was coming to an end, but so far the wintry weather had not, thank God. I usually looked forward to the warmth returning, the work picking up to occupy my time, but not this year. Now I would rather be stuck in a never ending Winter, as long as Caitlyn was with me.

For the next few days every time I looked for her I'd find her with her nose in one of the journals. She was enjoying them so much that I was glad I had decided to share them with her. She seemed oblivious to the raging storms and freezing temperatures outside, which meant they wouldn't be foremost in her mind when she made her decision to stay, or go.

I did notice that whenever I came into the room, she closed the journal she was reading and gave me her full attention. It made me feel like I was important to her and I loved her even more for it.

Caitlyn

Being eager to get to the journal entries about Jacob's birth, I hurried through the next six months of Kathryn's account. There were a few entries during this time that were filled with the wonderment of having a life growing inside her body. Feeling his first kick the end of May was especially poignant. As her belly grew and his movements increased Kat's excitement escalated and she shared her joy with her loving husband.

I noticed that even though the Winter was approaching there were no words of gloom in her entries. With her mind on impending motherhood all her past fears were forgotten. Her apprehension about the birth were revealed in her next entry.

November 29, 1852
The tightening sensations in my abdomen have been quite intense today, I'm sure my time is near. I remember my mother's words, how the pain of childbirth is worth every scream, every tear, when you hold your child for the first time. I feel apprehensive. How can you prepare for something that you've never experienced? You can't. Thank God Hattie's close by. She's gone through it twice and still speaks as if she'd love more children. It must be bearable. This thought gives me reassurance.

December 2, 1852
Nothing could have prepared me for the birth of my little Jacob, but my mother was right, all the pain had been worth this perfect boy I hold in my arms. He takes after his father, long for a newborn, according to Hattie, and already I see the tiny dimples in his cheeks when he twists up his face wanting to nurse. I never realized how much I could love him. Thank you Jake for giving him to us, and for the wonderful

Grandfather Clock you surprised me with on the day of Jacob's birth. The chimes remind me of my own childhood and the clock my parent's had in our home. I love it Sweetheart.

Again I have to thank God for the blessings of Hattie, I don't think we would have made it without her help. She did what had to be done and saved us. When I told her I named, my baby Jacob, Hattie said it was real nice to have a little son named after his father. I grasped her hand and told her his name is Jacob Samuel. I could tell she was moved when her eyes filled with tears. Hattie will never know how much she means to me even if I were to tell her everyday of our lives.

Kathryn's first journal ended on December 31st. Her first month of motherhood filled page after page with the wonderment of a first child, and according to Kat, he was the most perfect baby in the world.

Her second journal picked up in January 1853 and covered the next five years which ended with the birth of Jacob's sister Emily in December of 1857. I so enjoyed reading about Jacob as a young child, all his firsts as he grew from infant to toddler, and Kathryn loved to embellish on all the details. I found myself laughing along with her at some of the adventures the happy family shared.

She also continued updates of the progress being made on the new cabin Jake was building for her. It was quite large compared to their current home and would have separate bedrooms for Jacob and Emily, besides the huge bedroom for the two of them. Jake told her he wanted a large playground for them to enjoy. She loved the new cabin, her only complaint was that it was so far away from Hattie, at least a 15 minute ride on horseback in good weather.

There was one disturbing entry the beginning of December '57' that I couldn't wait to question Jacob about when he came home for lunch.

December 3, 1857
That nasty man was back again, he came in with the other workers. He has family in the South and doesn't like the idea of Negroes living so close to my family which he made abundantly clear with his stupidity

and foul mouth. He pushed me too far this time and I intended to put him in his place.

Poor Hattie was trying desperately to get me to go inside, "think of the baby," she told me, as she grabbed at my arm trying to get me to go in and leave her to deal with the fool alone. That man had the audacity to back hand her and knock her to the ground for touching me, which sent me hurrying into the cabin, not to hide of course, but to get my bow and arrow.

When I stepped back out on the porch I saw his raised hand ready to slap her again and I put an arrow right through it. By this time the commotion had men running around like chicken's with their heads cut off. Jake showed up just in time to save the bastard because my next arrow was aimed at his heart and I would have fired without a second thought. No one was going to hurt my friend while I stood by and did nothing.

I finished up the rest of the second journal and stopped, still all worked up by the one entry. I was happy that her second child, a girl, had been born without complications on December 23rd, Hattie by her side the entire time. Kathryn was thrilled with her perfect little family.

Jacob

When I got home for lunch Caitlyn was waiting, with food on the table, and ready to pounced on me for the details about one of the entries in my mother's second journal. When she told me which one she was talking about I couldn't help but chuckle a little. It was a great story and over lunch I shared it with her.

"My father hired some men to help with the apple harvesting and one of the men who worked with them was a bigoted idiot," I began. "My father had warned him not to come back if he couldn't keep his mouth shut but he showed up on the day in question and butted heads with my mother over the close proximity of the Williams family and my parent's homes."

"You've got to understand, Caitlyn, it was really rough for Negroes back then, and there had been some trouble a couple of times directed at Samuel and Hattie Mae. They didn't have to worry about the plantation owner that they ran away from because my father had paid off their indenture and they were free, but that didn't stop the prejudicial behavior by some people."

Getting back to the entry, I continued, "Anyway, this man decided he was going to put Hattie in her proper place, according to his ideals. When my mother went to her defense, Hattie tried to get her to go in the cabin to keep my mother out of danger. My mother was in her last month of pregnancy at the time and Hattie wanted her to think about the baby and remove herself from any possible danger. Trying to steer my mother, by taking her arm and turning her towards the cabin, the man saw her touching my mother and decided to slap Hattie. This was a big mistake on his part."

"Caitlyn, you know how my mother felt about Hattie from reading her journals and there was no way she would allow anyone to harm her friend. My mother was also a marksman with her bow and arrow. She could hit a knot hole on a tree from 50 yards. When she saw this man, arm raised, ready to slap Hattie again, she took aim and put her arrow dead center in his hand."

"When my father arrived on the scene he told the man he was lucky to be alive and threw him off the property, telling him he would deduct the cost of the arrow from any wages he was owed."

With a big smile on her face, Caitlyn said, "I love your parents Jacob."

"Me too, Sweetheart. I told you they were great. I always knew they loved me, even when I got into trouble, which did happen occasionally."

After lunch Caitlyn informed me that it was time for her to get serious about learning to shoot the bow and arrow. My mother's expertise giving her the incentive to master this task. Truthfully, I had been remiss in her lessons since her first attempt which almost resulted in an additional hole being added, in a most painful manner, to the chest area of my body, but I agreed we could give it another try. Hopefully this endeavor wouldn't be the death of me, or any of the livestock.

Caitlyn

Jacob's instructional abilities with archery are slightly lacking. I wish his mother were alive to teach me, I'm sure she would have had more patience. I didn't wound or kill anyone, and only one of my arrows went a little wild causing a bit of concern for Daisy, the milk cow's well-being. Jacob informed me, chuckling nervously, that maybe I should continue working with sticks that didn't have sharp tips on them. He's lucky that I didn't have my bostaf with me at the time.

With him home in the cabin for the rest of the day I decided to give the journals a rest and enjoy his company. Even his good-natured ribbing about my lack of ability with a bow and arrow didn't hinder my pleasure of him. I did, however, get great satisfaction from his look of fear when I told him I would do much better tomorrow at my next lesson.

The following morning Jacob told me he would be working in the root cellar, adding the shelves I'd suggested were needed down there. Truthfully I believe he came up with this plan to avoid another archery lesson. When he went down the stairs, with tools in hand, I grabbed the 3rd journal and headed to my favorite reading spot and began reading at January 1858.

Kathryn's entries for the first 6 months were centered around her new daughter, Emily, with a lot of references to Emily's big brother, Jacob. From what I read little Jacob adored his baby sister and from the baby's big smiles whenever he was near, it was obvious the feeling was mutual.

The entries beginning July 15, 1858 made me realized how intelligent Kathryn was. Up to this point there was no reference to her education and I hadn't known that for a women from her century she was highly educated.

July 15, 1858
I look at my son and realize, that in this wilderness where we live, the only education he'll be able to get is from me. Jacob will be 6 years old this November and it's about time I put my education to good use and begin teaching the boy how to read and write. I had ordered some of the books I would need for this task and had slate and chalk on hand. I know he won't like sitting down long enough to learn his letters but he's going to have to just accept it.

This afternoon when we were in the middle of his first lesson Hattie knocked on the door with one of her delicious Sweet Potato Pies in hand. When she saw us at the table immersed in writing the letter A repeatedly, she questioned what we were doing. I informed her that I was teaching Jacob to read and write. She looked at me with a longing in her eyes, and asked, "Will you teach me too, Miss Kat?"

After everything Hattie had done for me over the years I was thrilled with the idea of being able to do something for her that would enhance her life like reading could. Smiling at her without saying a word, I slid a slate and chalk to an empty place at my table and she sat down. I've never had such a rapt pupil and by the time the first lesson was over Jacob, and Hattie, could write an A in capital, and lower case letters, knew how to make it's sound and could name a number of things that started with that letter. I gave them both a big A for their progress.

Hattie asked if she could take home the slate and chalk to practice with and I happily agreed pleased with her enthusiasm.

August 10, 1858
My students have mastered the last letter of the alphabet today. Both of them can now write their names, and many three and four letter words. I'm quite proud of both of them.
I also found out from Isaac that his momma was teaching their daddy and both her boys at home every night. She sits with them after supper and redoes the lessons I teach her earlier in the day. When she had

asked me to write Samuel's and her son's names for her I had no idea that she was teaching them too. I am especially proud of Hattie Mae.

Jacob is proving to be quite intelligent. His mind is like a big sponge and once he learns something it's absorbed, and retained. He loves to read words to me and his father, off anything that has lettering on it, and is excelling beyond my expectations. His grasp of numbers has come naturally since he was just a little thing, and when asked how old he was, would hold up two chubby fingers and say, "One, two." Very clever indeed!

I enjoyed reading about the progress they were all making over the next few months. Kathryn's schooling techniques seemed to be very effective and by Christmas they were all reading books of varying aptitudes. Kathryn gave them each a special book as a Christmas presents.

During the Winter of '59,' the harsh weather left very little to do except concentrate on everyone's education. Even Jake did his part, going over the farm's books with Samuel who could now read them and help with some of the easier math involved. These skills seemed to increase Samuels pride in himself.

The next entry that grabbed me was on April 30th. Jacob had mentioned this incident and I was anxious to hear Kathryn's retelling.

April 30, 1859
The weather had been abnormally warm for the beginning of April in these parts. The sun was bright, and the ray's warmth felt wonderful on my face. The snow was melting at a higher rate than usual for this time of year, and taking advantage of the beautiful day, I decided to take the children for a walk by the stream, Snowball along for the exercise.

Jacob, being the rambunctious little boy that he was, insisted on my attention to show me his latest trick. which took my eyes off Emily for just a moment. After applauding his talent, I turned back to find my daughter gone. Panic coursed through me when I spotted her tiny figure heading towards the edge of the half frozen stream. I ran to her, and just before reaching her, she turned and gleefully ran back in the opposite direction.

When I turned to follow I heard the cracking sound, instantly knowing that I had made a grave mistake. Without any warning I crashed through the ice and plunged under the frigid water. Icy needles stabbed into my skin, the pain intense, as I struggled against my heavy sodden clothing trying to reach the surface for air.

When I was finally able to get my head above the surface I called out to Jacob to take care of his sister. I continued to struggle, my clothing like anchors, pulling me back down. I tried to grab at the edges of the ice to keep above the water, but my hands slipped as the ice kept cracking around me. Snowball was on the bank barking frantically, trying to get to me as I was pulled under again, and again, from the weight of my clothes.

Thank God, Jake had come home for lunch, and when Hattie Mae had told him about our walk he decided to come and join us. When he heard Jacob's young voice screaming for me and Snowball's alarming bark he took off running in our direction, and with Bear by his side, arrived just minutes after the incident had occurred. Hearing his panicky voice calling my name, I fought my way to the surface once more, knowing this was the last of my strength as I sunk back down under the water.

The next thing I felt was a powerful splash next to me as Bear jumped in. I can remember feeling myself being pulled up by the back of my jacket and dragged to the bank, then my world went black.

When I woke up I found Hattie sitting next to my bed, holding the Bible that she was now fond of reading. She called out to Jake who rushed to my side, Emily in his arms and Jacob peeking around from behind him. They all stood there just staring at me with tear filled eyes, causing mine to fill. I didn't know at the time that I had been unconscious for over a week.

By the time they had gotten me back to the cabin my skin was cold, hard, and blue, my breathing shallow and my heartbeat almost *nonexistent. Jake thought I was dead, but Hattie worked on me, warming me with vigorous massage, ordering Jake to build up the fire, and get her what she needed to bring life back to my almost frozen body. She managed to get my blood moving through my veins, saving me again. God bless you Hattie, I wasn't ready to leave my family.*

When Jacob came upstairs from the root cellar he found me sobbing. When I told him where I was in the journal he understood my tears.

"That was a scary time for our family," he said, and continued, "I remember feeling responsible because my mother was watching me when my sister went out on the ice. My father tried to reassure me that it was an accident and that I wasn't to blame, but until she woke up and told me the same thing, I didn't believe him."

After reading so much about his parents, and feeling like I knew them, I was curious about their deaths and with emotion in my voice asked, "How did they die Jacob?"

With the look of sadness that came to his face I was afraid I had made a mistake in my question, but when he spoke I knew he was ready to tell me.

"They were on a train heading out on the trip of a lifetime, according to them," he said. I could see him remembering as he went on, "They had planned the trip for a long time and were so excited, talking about the many stops they would make along the way. The train ride was only the first leg, to be followed by a ship across the ocean to England. My mother had always wanted to visit England, her ancestors were from there.

"The train never made it to the boat. It derailed and most of the passengers on board were killed. They told me that my parents hadn't suffered, the impact killed them instantly. They found them together," he finished, his pain at their loss evident.

"You know Caitlyn, as much as I would have loved having at least one of them alive, I'm glad they went together. It would have been unbearable for either of them to be without the other."

I walked to Jacob and wrapped my arms around his waist, feeling his tighten around me. Words weren't necessary, our embrace was enough.

After a couple of minutes I felt his lips brush my forehead, then say, "Do you want to see your new shelves?"

I answered, "Yes," but was reluctant to leave his arms, which seemed to be mutual because he didn't let go. Finally arm in arm we walked to the cellar door.

Carrying the lantern, Jacob led the way. The first thing I noticed was that the railing on the stairs was sturdy. I had mentioned once that it was loose and I was afraid to lean against it for fear of falling, so he fixed it.

When we got to the floor I looked around and was pleased with the addition of a double stack of shelves on the far wall where before there was none. Jacob had even moved the barrels and burlap bags up off the floor.

"When the weather warms up, we'll come down and I'll help you set it up the way you want, but right now it's freezing down here, so let's go back up," he told me.

When we got back upstairs I made lunch and when we were finished Jacob offered, with trepidation in his voice, to give me another archery lesson. I decided to give him a break for today and told him I really wasn't up for it. When I heard his exaggerated sigh of relief I almost changed my mind.

Since Jacob was occupied with farm paperwork I went back to the journals enjoying the entries for the rest of '59' and most of the '60's. When I got to November 1860 I found the entry for the day Jacob had first traveled to the future.

November 26, 1860
Today was a sad day for our entire family. Old Bear died peacefully in his sleep last night and has left a hole in all of our hearts. Jacob took it the hardest, running off and being gone for hours. Bear has been

his constant companion for his whole life and I realize how much he'll miss his friend.

Jacob was gone for so long that I was starting to get concerned about his absence and was just going to send Jake out looking for him when he returned. He stayed in his room for the rest of the day, thankfully he allowed Grizzly in with him. We had added Grizzly to the family from the last litter and the little guy was always following Jacob and Bear when they'd let him.

My heart has been extra saddened by the loss of Old Bear, I was devastated when we lost my precious Snowflake a year ago and can still visualize her beautiful brown eyes in my mind, but Bear saved my life and I'll always remember him with love and gratitude. These two Newfoundlands were the first I'd ever seen and even though I wasn't pleased by them at first, I've grown to adore the breed. We'll always have at least two in our family.

Closing the journals for the day, I got up and walked over to the couch calling the two big monster dogs that were laying on the living room floor. They both jumped up and came to me, giving me slobbery kisses as I petted and told them both how handsome they were.

Jacob closed his farm ledgers and joined us on the couch, saying, "I bet I can guess what your reading about."

"Your mother sure loved the dogs, and I can see why. I don't know what I would have done without them when you were buried in the snow. They're worth their weight in gold as far as I'm concerned."

"Maybe it's time we got a pretty little female pup just for you," Jacob suggested.

"Sounds like a plan to me," I responded giving him a big kiss.

Jacob

We were into the third week of March, the cold still relentless. Caitlyn had finished the third Journal and was almost through the forth which covered the years of the Civil War. I was only 9 years old when it started and didn't understand a lot of what was happening at the time. Our family had moved into our new cabin just before Christmas in 1860 and the excitement, over having my own room and all the new property to explore, that I didn't even think about any war, besides I had just found my secret cave in October and that whole thing had my mind spinning.

Caitlyn had read about Isaac joining the war and how upset the Williams family and my parents were about his safety. Her and I discussed the war after dinner one night while we sat together on the couch.

"I remember in '63' that Isaac turned 18 and enlisted to fight," I began. "Hattie Mae and Samuel were worried sick about him going down South. Their memories of the place were filled with fear, sadness, and pain and the thought of their boy being exposed to the hatred scared them half to death. The worst thing was not hearing from him for over a year."

"When Isaac finally returned home in '65' he brought back a young slave woman and her sister. Actually they brought him home, he had gotten shot while he was helping them escape and if they hadn't stayed with him he probably would have died before getting here. You've met them Caitlyn, it's Lizzy and Ellie, Hattie's daughters-in-law."

"Lizzy helped Hattie Mae nurse Isaac back to health and those two fell head over heels for each other. It also left Ellie and Henry alone a lot and cupid's arrow got them too. Hattie was pleased with both matches because she had fallen in love with both girls almost instantly. I think she felt a kinship with them because of the similarities in their lives."

"My parents had deeded over our old cabin and 50 acres of land to Samuel as payment for all his work on the new cabin. Hattie Mae had always loved the kitchen in my mother's cabin so they moved into the bigger cabin leaving theirs empty for Isaac and Lizzy when they married. Everything just seemed to fall into place."

I loved watching Caitlyn's face when I related these stories, her eyes gave away every emotion she felt and right now they were sparkling. I felt like I could drown in her eyes. I couldn't stop myself from taking her chin in my fingers and kissing her.

When the kiss ended I noticed that look of devilment in her eyes as she said, "What was that kiss for Jacob? Are you trying to get out of my archery lesson tomorrow?"

Laughing I answered, "No Sweetheart, if you want a lesson tomorrow I'll put on my suit of armor and give you your lesson, but right now I'm thinking about a different type of lesson I'd like to give you, upstairs."

She stood up, and smiling slyly, extended her hand to me.

Caitlyn

By the end of March I had finished all six of Kathryn's journals and felt like I knew Jacob's parents personally. Their passion for each other, their family, and their friends had been so strong that it was hard to believe they were gone. Kathryn had many entries in her final journal about the plans being made for the future trip that had ended their lives. Her excitement about the new adventure that she would one day soon share with her husband was evident.

I also noted a lot of entries is reference to Jacob's loneliness. She had noticed his absences over the years during the Spring and Autumn when he was coming to see me and wondered where he would go. One of the last entries she wrote showed her concern for his happiness.

April 25, 1878
My son disappeared again today. He's been going somewhere all week, leaving for hours and nobody knows where he is. He's an adult and I have no right to ask what he's up to, but I've noticed a happiness in his eyes that only seems to appear when he goes on these mysterious trips of his, which leads me to believe a woman is involved.

Jacob has grown into a magnificent man and deserves to be happy. Our home here in the mountains is wonderful, but lonely when you don't have someone to share it with. The selection of women available for him to chose from is extremely limited and he doesn't get away from here often enough to have an opportunity to meet a woman elsewhere.

My greatest prayer, Dear Lord, is that Jacob finds the love of his life and can know the same passion I've shared with his father.

Closing Kathryn's final journal my thoughts were on Jacob. He was a magnificent man. Strong, compassionate, loving, I could go on for days with his attributes, but the thing that I felt the strongest was my love for him. I would never be able to leave him and I had to put my guilt about my family back home aside, and tell him. Maybe tomorrow on the way home from our outing would be a good time.

Jacob had told me that he wanted to get another puppy, for my protection he had said, and he wanted to have Griz sire it. We were going to take Griz to the breeder in the morning because they had a brown female in heat. I was very excited about getting out of the cabin for a few hours and seeing another part of the mountains. I didn't know how the whole breeding thing went but I'm sure Jacob would explain it to me on the way.

Jacob

This had been the coldest Winter that I can remember, but with Caitlyn here to help keep me warm, I was a happy man. Instead of the months, seeming to be endless, they were flying by. The beginning of April brought slight signs that Spring was approaching, but instead of being happy as was the norm, I was miserable.

Caitlyn still hadn't made up her mind, at least not in words, as to whether she was staying, or not. After getting a taste of how wonderful life could be when you shared it with your soul mate, I might lose her and thinking about it made it hard to breath. It was the little things, like her laughter, her voice as she sang one of her favorite songs, just having her across from me at the table to share a meal, everything about her was special, and I never wanted it to end. I didn't even want to live, without her.

When I mentioned that I wanted to breed Griz, and get another puppy for her, she seemed very excited about the idea. I took that as a good sign that her thoughts were leaning towards staying. It was about an hour and a half ride to Harland and Molly's farm, with views of the mountains that showed off the majesty of this land that she would enjoy. If Caitlyn stayed I'd have to go visit Hans and see about getting her a camera.

We headed out right after breakfast, Bear looking forlorn when he was left behind. Griz must have sensed what was going on and was extra rambunctious. The ride was as beautiful as I had expected and I could see Caitlyn looking around in awe, her blue eyes darting back and forth as she pointed out different scenes. I watched as she made a little square with her fingers looking through it from different angles, I know wishing for her camera. I definitely had to go see Hans. .

While we were in route I explained the mating process to her and she informed me that she would feel uncomfortable watching so I assured her she could hang out with Molly until I got Griz settled and then her and I could explore the farm until things were done. This seemed acceptable and when we got there I introduced her to Molly and Harland and headed to the breeding barn with Harland.

Molly was a mountain farm woman through and through, even wore pants most of the time. Caitlyn seemed to take a liking to her immediately and I felt they would hit it off while I was introducing Griz to his mating partner who was a beautiful bitch, with a coat the color of copper. They were going to make beautiful puppies.

Before I could get back I saw Molly escorting another man and his dog back to the breeding barn and asked Molly if Caitlyn was still on the porch. "I hated to leave her sitting there alone, but she told me she'd be fine and would take a walk to the barn to see my horses," Molly informed me.

"I'll catch up with her there, Molly, she does love horses," I said heading for the barn.

As I came around the corner I noticed with disgust the Thomas brother's wagon by the far side of the barn. They ran a breeding farm further up the mountain that had the most deplorable conditions for the animals. They had been insulted and belligerent when I refused to sell them my dogs, but there was no way I would have allowed any of my animals to be left in their care.

With a feeling of unease I headed to the barn as quickly as I could. Entering the door I heard Frank's snarling voice say, "I think that bitch broke my nose, hold her."

I came around the corner just in time to see the two younger brothers holding a thrashing Caitlyn by her arms as Frank, blood running down his chin, backhanded her across the face. I went insane with anger and came up behind Frank, grabbing him by the back of his shirt and hurling him across the stall with so much force that the wall shook when he hit it. He just slumped to the ground and didn't move.

The two holding Caitlyn were so stunned by my demeanor that they were frozen in place. Never stopping my forward motion I roared, "Take your hands off my wife, now!"

They both let go at the same time and Caitlyn sunk to the floor, bringing her hand up to her bruised cheek in obvious pain. My fury was beyond control as I reached the brother closest to me and plowed my fist into his face, sending him reeling backward where he collapse not far from where Frank still laid.

The last brother standing, decided he was going to be brave and pulled a knife, bringing a sneer to my face. I was all over him before he could even move his hand, bringing my right elbow around and catching him in the side of the head, then bringing my left fist up and slamming it into his chin. I heard the knife fall as he crumpled, blood and drool pouring out of his mouth.

Spinning around, looking for my next opponent, I heard Caitlyn call my name. Her voice brought back my sanity and I rushed to her, asking, "Are you all right, Baby?"

When she raised her face to me I saw the son-of-a-bitch's hand print on her cheek, and the look of panic in her eyes at what she saw behind me. Spinning around I found that Frank had regained consciousness and was coming towards me intent on bringing the shovel he had raised, down on my head.

I ran at him, plowing into his chest and pushing him away from Caitlyn as he brought the shovel down missing us both. I was out of control by this point and started beating the hell out of him, my bloody fist making contact with his face, over and over.

Feeling something touch my back, I spun again ready to attack my next adversary and found Caitlyn, tears in her eyes begging, "Please stop Jacob, your going to kill him." I could tell from her expression that she was terrified from the violence I was displaying.

I pulled her into my arms, my whole body still pulsating with pent-up rage. I heard her say, "I'm alright Jacob, just get me out of here, please."

We walked out of the barn and back to the porch where Molly, noticing that something was wrong, jumped up and came to us. I told her she needed to send a couple of men to the barn to clean up the mess I left in there and drag the trash to the sheriff.

When Molly heard what had happened she did as I asked, sending two of her men to the barn, then apologized to me, telling me that she hadn't even know that the Thomas' were on her land. When her farm hands rode past with the three brothers in the back of the wagon they laid in a heap still unmoving. I hoped it was a permanent condition.

I went in Molly's house and got myself cleaned up, washing the Thomas brother's blood off. My hands were a little bashed up, from Frank's face I thought, smiling to myself, but that was the extent of my injuries. I walked back out to the porch and looked at Caitlyn.

She was sitting quietly, holding a cool cloth to the side of her face. When she lowered it I could see the bruise and a fresh wave of fury seethed through me. Seeing her watching me I tried to calm down, not knowing what she was thinking. She had seen me lose control and I hoped I hadn't scared her in some way, and prayed that she realized I would never physically hurt her.

After about 30 minutes Harland brought a subdued Griz back to us and we headed for home. For the first half of the trip we rode in silence, my apprehension growing until I heard her say, "I'm sorry Jacob, I should have known better than to go walking in an unfamiliar place alone like that. You could have been hurt and it would have been my fault."

"Caitlyn, you were hurt," I told her, going on I said, "I'm afraid I scared you with my violent behavior, but I'll never stand by and let anyone harm you."

"You were pretty scary Jacob, but I know you'd never hurt me. You kicked ass, I was really impressed."

Turning, I saw her looking at me like I was her hero and a feeling of relief flooded me. "I'd give my life for you Caitlyn, you should know that by now."

Leaning against my side she said, "I do."

Putting my arm around her we rode the rest of the way home without talking. When we neared the cabin I could see Bear looking out the window waiting for our return. My little family was home safe.

It took about two weeks for the bruise on Caitlyn's cheek to fade completely. Every time I saw it I was reminded of how easily something could have happened to her and I was afraid she thought about it too, making her think twice about staying.

The weather was growing warmer with each new day, and the signs of Spring were more obvious each day. Caitlyn still hadn't told me her decision and it was driving me crazy. I just couldn't lose her now.

Caitlyn

Looking out the kitchen window I could see the signs that Spring had arrived. Patches of melting snow were broken up by touches of green, with tiny hints of color, that promised the beauty of new life that came with this season. I could hear Jacob upstairs, rummaging about, getting ready for the day.

When he finally appeared downstairs, giving me a weak smile, he sat and ate his breakfast in silence. His mood this morning subdued, obviously his mind preoccupied with thoughts that he cared not share with me. When he finished eating he stood, announcing he had work to do, and with a quick kiss to my cheek, he left the cabin.

Standing in the kitchen, I watched him through the window as he walked to the wood pile. Lifting the heavy axe he assailed the wood like a man possessed, his shirt soon glued to his upper body by the physical exertion, until he finally just removed it.

I could have stood there all day watching the play of his muscles, wondering to myself how someone so strong and powerful, could also be so gentle, so tender. I had to finally pull myself away from the window because I knew if I continued watching him, bad mood or not, I'd go out in the yard and attacked him. I was crazy in love with this man.

I busied myself with household chores hearing him as he continued his assault on the wood. Glancing out again, I was just in time to see him as he let out a roar and flung the axe away. He took a few steps, standing with his back to me, hands on his hips, staring off in the direction of the mountains. There was something tearing him apart inside and I was going to find out what it was, now.

Grabbing a glass of water for him I went out to where he was standing. When I got close I called his name. Swinging around, he stood there looking at me with pain filled eyes. "What's wrong Jacob?" I asked.

"Just look around you Caitlyn, you can leave whenever your ready," he declared with grief in his voice. "If I had some dynamite I'd go to the waterfall and blow the damn cave up, then you'd have to stay," he rambled on, "I might have to spend the rest of my life begging you to forgive me, but at least you'd be here."

Not being able to stand his pain anymore, I walked to him, wrapping my arms around his waist. "I'm not going anywhere Jacob," I said against his chest, hearing his heartbeat. "The only way I will ever leave you is if God takes me back."

Taking my face in his hands he turned it up towards his and looked in my eyes. "Are you sure?" he asked. "It's a hard life here and I can't give you what your used to in your world, no matter how hard I'll try."

"Jacob, You're the world where I belong."

Holding me in his arms he said, "You'll never be able to see your family again."

"I know that Jacob, and my guilt at just walking away from them has kept me from saying out loud that I'm staying, but if I left, I'd never see you again and that would be unbearable." I went on, "I love you, you're my family now, and hopefully in the years to come we can add to it."

He lifted me off the ground, bringing my lips to his, and kissed me with such tenderness I thought I'd melt like the snow, then he spun me around with joy, his mood doing a complete three-sixty.

Finally setting my feet back on the ground, he said smiling, "My arms are killing me, I'm glad I don't have to chop any more wood for a while."

Poking him in his sore bicep, I turned and took off running for the cabin, laughingly calling over my shoulder, "I guess I'll have to be on top."

He immediately followed me in hot pursuit, catching me at the door and snatching me up in his arms, letting out a little groan of pain. "Only if you want to," he said, as he continued up the stairs where we stayed for most of the afternoon.

Caitlyn

Waking to the feel of Jacob's hands gently stroking my body, and the fresh scent of peppermint, was the way I wanted to wake up everyday. Laying there with my eyes closed feigning sleep, I luxuriated in the sensations he was stirring in me. Holding back the moans that threatened to escape me, I heard him say, "You can open your eyes Love, I know your awake. The responses I'm getting from your body right now are not the ones I get when your sound asleep."

Opening my eyes I looked into his, that look of assurance he had when he knew he was right staring back at me. God, he was so sexy. I watched as he moved down and started placing warm feathery kisses on my belly, setting off chills that traveled through me like an icy fire. The man definitely knew where all my buttons where.

When he was finished with his focus on my lower regions he started inching his way up my body, pausing at my breasts to show his adoration for them. I could feel his desire throbbing against my legs as he continued his upward momentum, praying as I opened up to him that he wouldn't stop.

As he entered me he finally brought his lips to mine and I could taste the peppermint in his mouth. Using my tongue I stole the last little piece as our kisses deepened with each of his slow deliberate thrusts. My body felt alive with ecstasy, the pleasure so intense I pulled him in deeper as we both surrendered to the waves of delight surging through our bodies.

Laying on top of me, he lifted on his elbows and caressed my face with his hands, the spasms still coursing through me as he kissed me tenderly, and said, "I love you Caitlyn."

Looking in his eyes as I laid there beneath him enjoying his touch, I said, "I love you too, Jacob, with my whole heart."

We laid together on our bed just holding each other, neither wanting to move. Unfortunately nature had a way of ruining things sometimes and I had to get up to relieve an over-filled bladder.

When I returned we decided to get our day started, so we both dressed and headed down for breakfast. The living room was flooded with bright sunlight shining in from the big window near the beams of the ceiling. It looked like it was going to be a perfect day for our picnic. It had sure started out perfect.

Jacob

After weeks of dreading the coming of Spring, life was perfect, Caitlyn was staying, she had told me yesterday. Lying in bed last night, she proved to me that even though she loved and missed her family back home, she loved me more, and could never just walk away from us. Holding her in my arms I asked her to be my wife.

Pausing just long enough to cause me concern, she turned that wicked little smile of hers on me and said, "Yes Jacob, I want to be your wife for the rest of my life." I wanted to shout to the rooftops. We planned a trip to the city the next weekend to make everything official.

Caitlyn asked if I would take her on a picnic tomorrow, so she could say goodbye to her family. She felt like she needed to do this as a kind of closure to her future self. She should have known I'd take her to the ends of the earth to make her happy. I made slow passionate love to my future wife and we fell asleep in each other's arms, contented and spent.

Waking up this morning and continuing where I left off the night before, I woke her with a gentle touch, caressing her and bringing her as much pleasure as I was capable of. From the satisfied look on her face when I was done, I think I did a pretty good job.

When we finally got out of bed we found that the day was ideal for our planned outing. The sun was shining bright, the birds and flowers all waking up for spring, and the dogs were barking rowdily. Okay, the dogs barking wasn't ideal, but they seemed to be excited and raring to go along. Caitlyn packed a basket of food for us, throwing in a little treat for the dogs, and grabbing a blanket to sit on, we headed out, hand in hand.

It was a pleasurable 20 minute walk to the waterfall, Caitlyn and I just enjoying the togetherness. Bear and Griz took off on an adventure of their own leaving us peacefully alone. Caitlyn was full of energy and started running ahead of me, laughing when I started after her. She had a pretty good head start because I purposely held back so I could enjoy the view of her swaying body. The basket and her hips, moving in opposite directions brought to mind other things we could do on that blanket, besides sit.

I heard her terrified scream before I even saw the charging bear. A monster in size he had come out of nowhere, crashing through the brush, and was on her with such ferocity, grabbing hold of the back of her jacket with his powerful jaws, and shaking her like a rag doll. He dropped her and she curled into a tight ball, her whimpers of fear and pain almost drowned out by his snarling growls. He batted at her, again and again, with his huge paws and I could see patches of her blood seeping onto her clothing.

My fury exploded inside me, and I went berserk. Throwing my arms up in the air, I roared with all the anguish I was feeling as I rushed towards them, predator and prey. Momentarily forgetting Caitlyn, the bear, standing on his hind legs, rose to his full powerful height meeting my challenge with his mouth wide open, and vibrating with his roars. I could see dried blood staining most of his one leg and realized that besides being on a rampage, he was wounded. A really bad combination.

"Caitlyn," I shouted over and over, directing it at the bear, but calling out to her at the same time. The bear didn't attack right away, his muscular body erect, sizing me up and trying with all his might to intimidate. He also hadn't moved far enough away from Caitlyn, and was still blocking my path to her. I saw the slight movement of her head as she peeked up at me, panic in her eyes.

Griz appeared, charging past me directly at the bear, fighting fiercely with protectiveness, and distracting it just enough for me to get to Caitlyn, and snatch her up. Carrying her I ran for the waterfall. If we could climb up to the ledge we could get in the cave and escape through the narrow passage. Running full out, I glanced back just in time to see the bear's powerful paw slamming into Griz's head, sending him flying out of it's way.

The bear began it's pursuit, picking up speed and gaining on us rapidly. He already had a taste of Caitlyn's blood and he wasn't going to give up what he considered his. I made it to the base of the waterfall and started the climb, not getting far before he was on us again. Pushing Caitlyn up and out of my arms I told her to move, climb, NOW. As she began her hurried ascent, I turned and faced the huge animal, ready to fight to the death to give Caitlyn enough time to climb to the cave.

I heard the fierce barking as Bear appeared behind the beast, attacking with vigor from the rear, and drawing his attention away from us again. The running water of the falls made the rocks slippery and as I rushed up the rock face I heard Caitlyn's panic cry as she slipped on the slick rocks and started sliding back down. When she was right next to me I reached out and grabbed her, pulling her up against me.

"I won't let you fall, Baby," I said, reassuring her.

I could see that her movements were painful and I cursed, with rage at myself, for allowing her to be harmed again. We made it to the opening of the cave before the bear caught up with us again. I pushed Caitlyn in and told her to go through. She turned, her tear filled eyes pleading, afraid of the unknown if she went in.

Looking directly in her eyes, my own demanding, I yelled at her, "Go!"

Doing as I said, she turned, and ran, just as I felt the searing pain of the bear's sharp fangs sinking into my arm, grabbing me, and forcefully jerking me back out. All my grief and torment came out in one word, as I bellowed her name.

Fate's Plan

"Destiny comes to pass"

Bronwyn

April 30, 2012

It has been almost a full 6 months that my sister, Caitlyn, has been in a Coma. After 3 months in Hospitals and a Nursing Home we moved her to my Grandparent's house and hired full-time Nursing Aides. It was easier on my Grandparents having her in their home, since one, or the other, of them was always visiting her in the facilities. My parents decided it would be best for Caitlyn, and my grandparents, for her to stay in New York for now. She had the best doctors, who even made House Calls here.

Every day we all sat vigil in her room, the one Caitlyn and I always shared when we visited, and talked, or read to her. She never moved, or made a sound, and at times I'd find myself quietly crying, missing my sister more than anything in the world. We were so close, best friends, always had been. We talked on the phone, or skyped daily and not having her to talk to, and laugh with, was the hardest thing I'd ever gone through.

The Physical Therapist had been here earlier, exercising Caitlyn and manipulating her still body. The Nurse's Aide was running late because of the horrendous storm raging outside, which included Tornado warnings. I was alone with her now, just sitting there, willing her with my mind to wake up. It wasn't working.

I picked up the latest J.W. Deppens novel, number one on the Best Seller's list, and started reading aloud. After a couple of chapters I laid the book back down and looked at my sister's still, unresponsive face. Leaning my head back and closing my teary eyes, I fell asleep.

Her tormented shrieks shocked me awake, out of my chair, and to her side. She was sitting up, her I.V. tube ripped out of her arm and dripping blood on her clothing, her eyes wild and terror filled, staring right through me. I tried to hold her but she batted my arms away. Emotional tears streamed down my face as I tried to allay her fears, telling her that she was at Grandma and Grandpa's house, that she was safe, but she was inconsolable.

I heard my grandparent's running up the stairs and was glad when they finally rushed into the room. I was scared, helpless about what to do to help my sister. My Grandmother rushed to Caitlyn, gathering her in her arms, talking softly, and soothing her with love filled words that only Grandmothers know. Caitlyn's screams gradually turned to sobs as she repeatedly called out to someone named Jacob, and mumbling something about a bear. She was totally disoriented and still didn't seem to know who any of us were.

Grandma told me to run downstairs and call the doctor, see what he wanted them to do. I hurried down and got the doctor on the phone, who told me he would send an ambulance to pick her up, and take her to the hospital where he'd meet us. When the paramedics arrived they sedated Caitlyn and transported her to the E.R. This was the beginning of a month long ordeal of doctor's visits, mental and physical therapy, and psychiatric consultations.

After the first two weeks the doctor's diagnoses was depression and he wanted to medicate her. She refused to take the meds. All she did was lay in bed and cry, repeatedly telling us this outrageous story about Jacob and the bear. The doctor's felt that in her weakened state her dreams had become reality to her, and that it would take time and counseling to help her regain her senses. It sounded to me like they were saying my sister was crazy and I didn't like it one bit. My parents wanted to take her home to Florida, but Caitlyn refused this too, getting agitated at the idea of leaving. She convinced them that she was starting to feel better and wanted to stay.

Finally, about the third week after waking up, she got out of bed and dressed, insisting on taking a walk to the valley, wanting to go alone. My Grandparent's were wary at first, but finally agreed as long as she didn't stay too long. Caitlyn seemed excited when she returned, but by that evening she was curled up in her bed again. It took about another week before she started to come back to us.

For the next month Caitlyn went nuts on her computer, working on something she preferred not to share. I was just happy to see her up and about, even smiling a little again, especially since I had to go home in a few days and get back to my life.

Caitlyn mentioned at dinner a couple of days later, which she actually cooked, another first, that she had gotten in touch with her old friend, Emily from college, through face book. Emily had invited her up to Black Brook in Clinton County, to meet her husband and see her new baby. My grandparents didn't seem thrilled with the idea, but after seeing how animated Caitlyn was they agreed it would be good for her to go spend time with her friends.

Two days later Caitlyn and I got in my car, and after a teary farewell to Grandma and Grandpa, headed to the car rental dealership where I was dropping her off to pick up a car. Being a bit suspicious about her motives for this trip, I decided to question her about her friend on the way.

After beating around the bush for a while she finally said to me, "Wynie, I need to make this trip. I'm not going to get into details with you about it. If you love me, you'll just let it be."

I did love her, and she seemed to be determined in her decision, so there was really nothing I could do. When we got to the Dealership I hung around till the paperwork was done, and she had her keys. We walked out to the car together and hugged tightly. I told her I loved her, and she told me back. With a promise to call in a couple of days, she got in the car and drove away, heading north.

Watching her leave, I said a little prayer, hoping she'd find what she was searching for.

Caitlyn

It's been a month since I've returned, and my determination to find out what had happened to Jacob was strong. Physically I was fine, mentally I was a wreak. My parents, Grandparents and sister walked around me on eggshells acting like at any minute I might crack. Maybe they were right, maybe I already had.

When I had been home for three weeks I finally convinced them to let me go for a walk to the valley alone, telling them I needed the fresh air and exercise. The late spring day brought warm sunshine and cool air that felt wonderful on my skin after being inside for so long.

When I got to the valley I was devastated by the path of destruction left by the tornado that had touched down on the day of my return. There were parts of the clearing that were untouched, but the area closest to the sheer mountain face was flattened, including the twin trees that had stood as the entryway. I spent the better part of an hour walking along the solid rock wall searching for the cave opening, finding nothing. Saddened, I decided to head home.

I hadn't gotten very far when my foot unexpectedly hit something hard under a pile of leaves. I dug around with my foot, trying to uncover whatever was under there, and saw a reflection on metal. Reaching down, and brushing away the rest of the leaves, I found my camera which had been buried there since November.

The leaves had given it some protection during the months but it was in pretty bad shape. I opened the back and popped out the memory card which appeared to be fine. Excitement filled me, remembering the last photo I had taken had been of Jacob standing between the trees. I rushed home and immediately inserted it into my computer, praying the whole time that the images hadn't been destroyed by the elements.

Photo after photo appeared on the screen until finally the last one was up. It was a beautiful shot, the identical twin trees tall and leafless, back-dropped by the rock wall. It looked just like my oil painting, but no Jacob.

In my mind I could envision him standing there, arms crossed, with that smile of his on his face. It was the first time I had seen him, but unfortunately my camera hadn't caught his image. I just sat there staring at the picture, and cried.

Having a bit of a relapse, due to my disappointment, I stayed in bed most of the next week, until today. Today I decided it was time to do something, find the truth that Jacob had existed, and what had happened to him the day of my return.

I sat at my computer and typed in Ancestryhunters.com. When the website came up I pulled up the search window and typed in Jacobs full name and his date of birth. I wasn't sure which city, but I knew we had been in the Adirondack mountains in upstate New York so I typed North Country, New York, U.S.A. next. When I was ready I hit the search button.

A list of Jacob Wilkinson's appeared in the results column and I started going through them one at a time, looking for details, that I knew, to verify that I had the right Jacob. In my first search I didn't find any so I narrowed down my search to the 1860 census, and Bingo, there he was. Jacob S. Wilkinson, age 7, relationship to head of house: son. His parent's names and ages were listed along with his sister, Emily, age 2.

I wasn't crazy, here they were, all of them, right here in front of my eyes. I wanted to shout with jubilation, gather my family and show them, see, I'm not crazy. Then realization set in. They didn't know any of these details, I could have picked any Jacob from the 1860's and said, here he is. It wouldn't prove anything to them, but it definitely proved it to me.

For the next month I barely left my computer chair, my obsession taking over. I performed search after search, sometimes coming up empty, and other times just getting some small bit of information that I could use to track down another small bit. Once in a while I'd hit pay dirt, and the excitement of this continued to fuel my determination to keep going.

By the end of May this is what I had discovered:

Jacob's sister Emily, which I already knew from my time with Jacob, had been married to Joshua Dunkleberry in 1880. Emily lived in Black Brook Township in Clinton County, New, York. She had one daughter, Matilda in 1888, at the age of 31.

Through census' I found out that Matilda married Michael Beck, date unknown, and had one daughter, Eliza in 1914, at the age of 26.

Eliza married Mathew Wagner, again date unknown, and had one daughter, Elizabeth in 1942, at the age of 28. This was a lucky find because if Eliza and her husband hadn't been living with her parents, I would have never found it.

I hit a dead end with the census info after that and there was no records of Jacob's death anywhere, I know because I searched, diligently.

I switched my search to Property Deeds, going all the way back to the early 1800's and found Jacob's father listed as owner of 1,000 acres until 1881, which transferred to Jacob S. in 1882. The cabin was located near the Adirondack Mountains in Ellenburg Township, Clinton County, New York.

With the deed showing plot numbers and an address on Laclair Road I was able to hunt down previous and current owners which uncovered an Elizabeth and Jonathan Deppens from1943, followed by Jacob W. Deppens in 2002, who I assume was their son. I was pleased that they had carried on the name with the first born male in four generations, and even more delighted with the possibility that the cabin had stayed in the family all these years.

I put away all my papers, keeping my current activities hidden from my sister and Grandparents, for fear it would upset them. Since they were out for the afternoon I decided to enter the kitchen for the first time since returning and prepare a nice dinner for the four of us, assured that this activity would please them to no end.

Clipped to the inside of my folder was the phone number for one, Jake Deppens that I had managed to get from an acquaintance of mine at the phone company, with much begging, and assurance that my source would never be revealed.

Tomorrow I would tell my family of my plans for the little trip I was taking to Black Brook to visit a friend of mine from college, let's see, who just had a baby. Yeah, that would do it.

Jake

Writer's block, that's what I had, no matter how hard I tried I just couldn't get these final chapters to come together. My Publishers were on my ass, hoping for the release of my latest novel before the holidays. If my focus didn't improve they could kiss that idea goodbye.

With the sound of the Grandfather clock bonging in the hour of 6:00 a.m., I realized I needed a break, the ample amounts of caffeine flowing through my bloodstream, thanks to guzzling coffee all night, was giving me the jitters. Getting up, I closed my laptop and stretched, then headed for the door. Maybe some fresh air would help clear my brain fog.

Stepping out on the porch, the early morning air crisp, I was greeted by the sight of the rising sun coming up between the mountains. No matter how many times I'd seen this view it was always balm for my senses. That feeling of deja vu flooded me again, most likely due to the fact that I'd been living in this cabin most of my life. I loved it here, rich with family history, there was even a picture of my three times great grandparents who'd built it, on the fireplace mantle.

Walking to the railing, I stood taking it all in, just breathing in the beauty. The sun was just peeking through the v of the mountains, shooting rays up into the sky and lighting the clouds above. The colors and textures of the vista were always changing, depending on the season. On this summer morning it was breathtaking as always, but my favorite season was Autumn, when the trees were in full color.

Letting my mind wander I thought back on all the time, as a child, I'd spent running around this magnificent property. Climbing trees, playing hide and seek, and just exploring, my dogs always by my side.

It's my home now, full time for the last 10 years, my parents tired of the isolation moved out giving it to me. The tranquility here an excellent working environment for my chosen career, that is until now. Over the past couple months I couldn't seem to concentrate, my words fleeting, it was making me mean. I can't say I was ever known for my excellent social skills, becoming almost reclusive during long writing phases, but now, even my dogs seemed to be avoiding me. I probably just needed some damn sleep.

On the way back inside a sudden idea for my main character struck me and I rushed over, opening my laptop. Sitting down, my fingers barely touching the keys, when the cabin phone started ringing. "What the Hell!" Who'd be calling this time of the morning. No one ever called me here, except on my cell, which was upstairs on my nightstand.

Ignoring it, I tried to get my thought into writing, the ringing phone going on and on, before at last coming to an end. My thoughts became words, flowing out of my fingers and onto the screen. The thrill, when an idea blossomed, taking over. Feeling this might finally bring an end to the arduous task this book had become, the ringing began anew. Furious with this intolerable interruption, I snatched up the receiver and yelled, "What?"

A feminine voice on the other end hesitating, then saying, "Sorry," and hanging up.

My anger high, I paced about, wondering now, who had been on the phone, and how did she get this number. Probably some damn reporter I thought, all ideas for my book pushed away by my fury. I hated the fame my writing had brought me, the infamous J.W. Deppens.

I was a good writer, my novels always hitting the top of the New York Times Best Seller's List, and I loved writing, always had my whole life, but the notoriety sucked. The constant nagging by my Publishers wanting me to do book tours, interviews, and photo shoots to promote my latest novel.

And the women, they seemed to find my aloofness attractive, throwing themselves at me at every opportunity. I did like women, loved them in fact, but the ones I always seemed to meet were either artificial, or overly aggressive, both turn offs as far as I was concerned, hence the reason I was still single. Ever since making People's Sexiest Men's list my life had become pure hell. The only place I could find peace was here, in my secluded cabin in the mountains.

Realizing, after all this contemplation, that my writing was done for the day, thanks to my mysterious caller, I turned off my laptop and headed out to the barn for a much needed workout. Maybe after pushing my muscles to the limit I'd be able to get some sleep, and try writing again later.

Caitlyn

Hearing the angry, "What?" caused me to stammer a meek apology, and cringing, I hung up the phone. My God, what was I thinking calling this man at 7:00 a.m.? I had been up since 3:00, trying to work up the courage to actually make the call in the first place, and hadn't realize just how early it still was.

I wasn't sure exactly what I had expected as I dialed the man's number, but his rude, barked out, one word question wasn't it. OK, I understand it's early, but the normal response when answering a phone was usually, "Hello," no matter what time of day.

Thinking to myself, it was probably best that the call had ended abruptly, given that I really wasn't sure what I would have said.

"Hello, my name is Caitlyn and I traveled back in time and met your Great-Great Uncle," I rehearsed.

Oh Yeah! That was gonna get me in the door—NOT! Deciding it was best to put a little more thought into what I was going to say before calling back, I went down to the restaurant for some breakfast.

When I finished I went on a sight-seeing tour of the quaint little town I was visiting. The scenery surrounding Ellenburg was beautiful and as I turned in the direction of the mountains chills rushed through my body as I realized that I had been here before, with Jacob.

I'll never forget how I had longed for my camera that day after seeing this gorgeous panorama. At the time it had been snow covered, the town much smaller, all built of wood, but the majesty of these mountains was unmistakable.

Heading back to the hotel I came up with a cover story that I felt might peak Mr. Deppens interest. Checking my watch, 11:00 a.m. not too early for a call, so I dialed his number. After about the 10th ring it was finally answered, "Who is it?" he snarled into the phone.

Without thinking and totally offended by his lack of manners, I snapped back, "My God, hasn't anyone ever taught you proper phone etiquette?"

After a brief pause he answered sarcastically, "Sorry, I'm not always this rude, usually I'm much worse. What do you want?"

Clearing my throat I began my sham, "My name is Caitlyn Jacobs, I'm a Genealogists researching the family history of Samuel and Hattie Mae Williams, and was hoping you might be able to help me."

Sounding a little less angry but still annoyed, he responded with, "And what makes you think that?"

"Well, your ancestors and the Williams' ancestors had a connection in the late 1800's and I was hoping you might be able to clear up a few facts that I've been unable to trace," sounded good to me, I thought.

"Listen Lady, I don't have time for these interruptions," he declared, "and even if I did, I'm not interested in collaborating with you," he finished, hanging up.

I was back to square one. Figuring another phone call would just piss him off further, I decided it was time for me to visit Mr. Deppens, face to face. I knew the location of his cabin, had the address and a map all pin-pointed, and being as anxious as I was to see it, I had to give it a try.

Tomorrow though, give him a little time to cool off. Grabbing my camera I headed back outside to capture those mountains. They were almost as beautiful on this bright Summer's day as they had been last Winter, 130 years ago.

Jake

Back at my computer, struggling to focus on the storyline, my mind kept returning to my pesky caller, Caitlyn Jacobs she had said was her name. Her motive for contacting me yesterday, a bit suspect. It could be the truth I guess, but I doubted it, something in her voice made me believe she was lying. Her voice though, was stuck in my head, the way she had snapped back at me, implying I was rude, was refreshing.

No one had every told me I was rude before, except maybe my mother, even when I was acting like a real ass hole. Everyone generally fawned over me, saying all the right things that they felt I wanted to hear, placating me. It was boring. Trying again to shake my wandering reflections, I returned my attention to my laptop, but my mind again drifted to my faceless caller, "I wonder what she looks like."

Thankfully the dogs interrupted these thoughts with actions indicating their need to go out. Walking to the door I opened it wide and said, "Go on boys, go run off some steam." The two big Newfoundlands leaped around me displaying their exhilaration at being set free, then took off. I returned to my chair, sat down, and stared at the blank screen.

All of a sudden I heard the dogs barking wildly and causing quite a ruckus. At first I figured they must have found some small animal to chase, a favorite pastime of theirs, but the howling continued and seemed to be centered in the wooded area within close proximity to the cabin. Feeling the need to investigate, I walked to the door, picked up my rifle, and headed out.

I didn't have far to go before finding the source of my dogs commotion. The two of them had her pinned against a tree, yapping and leaping around her like they had just found a new toy to play with. You could tell from their demeanor that they didn't find her a threat. As I approached, carrying my rifle at my side, she turned her attention to me. Her eyes widened as I got closer, and filled with tears of apparent fear.

Deciding to give her a little break I said, "They won't rip your throat out, unless I tell them to." Calling the dogs back I moved a little closer. Her stare was intense, her eyes an unusual shade of deep blue. I knew who she was before she spoke, but I inquired anyway, "Caitlyn Jacobs I presume?"

She just nodded her head, never taking her eyes off me.

"I don't remember inviting you, so what could I have possibly done to make you think you might be welcome here?" I asked contemptuously.

My question seemed to snap her out of her fear, and as her eyes narrowed she replied, "Mr. Deppens, I see your manners haven't improved a bit since yesterday."

I wanted to laugh, but instead I turned on my meanest face, bantering back, "Oh, I'm sorry milady, I didn't mean to insult your fine sensibilities."

We both stood there, playing the staring game, giving me the opportunity to really check her out. She was beautiful, her face captivating with those expressive blue eyes of hers, and with a body to match she looked like she could be trouble. I was enthralled.

Finally caving slightly I asked in my most gentlemanly manner, "Since your already here, trespassing I might say, what can I do for you Ms Jacobs?"

She relaxed, her angry face softening as she answered, "I really would appreciate a little of your time to see if you can help me with my research."

"Alright, you've got my attention, I'll give you half an hour, follow me." Finishing with, "I just made a fresh pot of coffee, will you join me for a cup?"

She actually smiled which caused a little jolt in me, then nodded her acceptance of my offer. I led the way, walking through the trees and holding back an occasional branch to keep them from slapping her in her pretty face.

My dogs seemed to be happy with our company, and bounced around us as we walked, almost tripping me up, which brought about a little chuckle from Caitlyn. Giving her a little sneer, I kept walking as I heard her ask, "What's their names?"

"The back one's Onyx, his coloring, with the white spot on his chest, reminded me of the stone, and the brown is Copper, just because it seemed right," I informed her as we continued on. I could see her playing with them as we walked, both dogs falling all over themselves with their enjoyment of her attention. Maybe I need a couple of Rotts, I thought.

When we stepped out into the clearing where the cabin was I turned to her and said, "Welcome to my home Ms. Jacobs." I continued walking, telling her, "You should consider yourself lucky, I don't invite many people here."

Getting no response I turned and found that she had stopped walking as soon as we had left the trees. The expression on her face was like pure joy at first, then turned to deep sadness, her eyes filling again with tears. She wasn't moving so I walked back to her, touching her arm to get her attention, "Are you all right, Ms. Jacobs?"

"Caitlyn, please," she stated, finally looking at me, "What a beautiful Cabin," she said smiling tentatively in my direction.

It was my favorite place in the whole world and for some reason it pleased me that she liked it. Thanking her for her compliment I lead her to the porch, up the steps, and to the front entrance. Opening the door I stood to her side so I could watch her reaction, after witnessing her impression of the outside, I was anxious to see what she thought of the inside.

A look of awe enveloped her face and again her eyes filled with tears, spilling down her cheeks. Her words threw me for a loop when I heard her whisper, "I thought I'd never see it again."

Caitlyn

The signs posted all along the road stated, "No Trespassing," which I had completely ignored and finding a weak spot in the fence I squeezed through and walked in the direction of the cabin. As I walked along I was overcome with a feeling of nervousness.

Making my way up the incline of the mountain I was suddenly surprised by the riotous approach of two monstrous sized Newfoundlands. I should have known he'd have dogs. They were beautiful, one black with a white patch on his chest and the other a redish brown, similar in appearance to Griz. They encircled me and backed me up against a tree. That's where I was when the man appeared.

At first I was struck to the core, seeing just his silhouette as he moved towards me. He was as tall, if not taller than Jacob, with broad shoulders and a lean body, but it was his gait, that swagger, that brought on the nostalgia causing my eyes to fill.

The physical resemblance to Jacob made me positive that this was his great-great nephew, Jake. He said something to me about the dogs not hurting me, which I found unnecessary, seeing as I wasn't afraid of them at all. They were big, but just as lovable as Bear and Griz had been.

He got closer giving me a chance to study his features. His hair, the same light brown shade as Jacobs, was cut in a shorter, more modern style. The parts of his face visible above his full beard were similar, you could see the strong family resemblance there. It was his eyes that really drew me, the blue turned on me now with anger, still had that rogue look that I found so attractive. This man was gorgeous, but he wasn't my Jacob.

His rude question, jarred me out of my perusal and ignited my ire. He wasn't a very pleasant man which was in total contrast to Jacob. After a little back and forth between us he seemed to give in a little and actually invited me in for coffee. This is what I had really come for, to see the cabin, see if it was the one I had lived in for 6 months of my life.

He lead the way, showing a gentlemanly side as he held back branches for me. Maybe he wasn't so bad after all. When we stepped out of the trees I got my first full view of the cabin, and stopped dead in my tracks.

There it was, weathered by age, but every detail as I remembered. My tears came again, filling my eyes. When Jake touched my arm, asking if I was alright, I managed to pull myself together and follow him to the porch. He stood to the side and opened the door and I babbled something as tears finally overflowed my eyes. I couldn't hold them back any longer.

Jake led me to a chair so I could sit, not seeming to know what to do about my emotional breakdown. I let my eyes follow him to the kitchen that was still full of antiques, but modernized with the latest equipment. I had spent a lot of time in that kitchen, the window over the sink looking out over the pathway leading to the barn, the natural stone floor, and the basic design, still the same.

Jake brought me my cup of coffee and sat across from me at the table, starting the conversation, "All right, tell me what's going on Caitlyn. When were you ever here before?" adding, "The truth this time, please."

I decided to start with a question, "Mr. Deppens, has anything ever happened to you in your life that you couldn't explain?"

"Call me Jake, and to answer your question, Yes, but apparently not to the extent that it's happened to you."

Giving him a little smile in appreciation of his understanding, I continued, "I'm going to start at the beginning and ask that you please let me finish before you throw me out." He agreed and I began.

"On November 7, 2012 I attained a head injury when lightening struck a tree next to me. When my grandfather found me I was unconscious, so he rushed me to the hospital where I was diagnosed in a coma." I stood up and began pacing as I continued, "I was in the coma for 6 months, well at least part of me was."

Jake gave me a quizzical look, tilting his head slightly, and said, "Go on."

Now came the hard part, the unbelievable truth. I took a sip of my coffee to calm me and kept going, "My Grandfather wasn't the only one who found me that day," I said, walking to the mantle, getting the picture of Jacob and his sister and bringing it back, handing it to him.

"Jacob Wilkinson was there, saw the whole incident as it unfolded. He picked me up and carried my unconscious body here." I raised my hands, circling them to make my point, then looked at Jake's face to determine his reaction, finding him listening intently.

I took this as a positive sign and went on, "For two days he cared for me until I came to. I was weak for a while, and my head hurt, but I was conscious, lucid."

My throat was dry so I walked back to the table, sat down, and took another sip of coffee before going on, "When Jacob told me where I was, and explained the events of that day, I didn't know what to think. It was all so mind-boggling, and having a level head I couldn't figure out how it could be possible."

Still trying to figure it out in my own mind, I asked Jake, "How can someone travel back in time?"

Jake sat there shaking his head, not sure how to answer me. Finally he asked, "What did the doctors say about all this?"

"They said it was a dream, my subconscious doing crazy things, and I might have eventually believed them if I hadn't done my research and found that Jacob had existed."

Explaining, I said, "I found him in the 1860 U.S. Census. Jacob Wilkinson, age 7, his parents, Jacob James and Kathryn Marie, and his sister, Emily, your Great-Great Grandmother."

Jake leaned forward in his chair now totally engrossed in my story so I continued, "How would I know these people if I hadn't been here? How would I know details about their lives that you can't find no matter how much genealogical research you do?"

Jake finally spoke, "What kind of details are you talking about?"

I stood, walking over to the mantle again, I picked up the picture of Jacob's parents and said, "This picture was taken in 1880, about a year before their deaths in a train derailment, and this beautiful clock, that was a gift to Kathryn by her husband the day Jacob was born."

"I could go on, tell you all about Samuel and Hattie Mae Williams, their two sons, Isaac and Henry. I met them all. Did you know that when they first arrived here they were run-away slaves and that your Great-Great-Great Grandfather gave them work and shelter? Kathryn even taught them to read," the more I talked, the more emotional I got.

"Did you ever read Kathryn's Journals?" I asked him, "I did, all six of them, they were the most fascinating books I've ever read."

"I've never found any journals," Jake said, then asked, "Were they here in the cabin?"

"Yes, in the bedroom closet upstairs, Jacob hid them there," I answered him.

"Show me where Caitlyn," Jake requested.

Leading the way, with Jake following closely behind, I went up the stairs to the bedroom, the one Jacob and I had shared. When I stepped in the room I was surprised by the sight of my oil painting of the twin trees hanging on the wall above his nightstand. I also couldn't help but smile when I notice the small tin of mints sitting next to his cell phone.

"You still have the picture?" I said, more to myself than in question.

"I've always loved that picture, there's something about it that draws you in. I don't know who the artist is, it's just the initials, CJ, and the year," he started.

"1882," I finished for him.

Comprehension dawned on him and he asked, "You painted this, Caitlyn?"

"Yes, and I gave it to Jacob for Christmas. He loved it. The first time I saw him he was standing between those trees."

Turning from the picture, and walking to the closet door, I pointed, and getting his nod to continue, I opened the door. Pushing the clothes on the left side out of the way, I saw the knot hole and stuck my finger in, hooking it in the wood and pulling out the panel in the wall. The journals were still there, all individually wrapped in oil cloth. I looked quickly to see if there was anything else there, but all I saw was the journals.

Turning to face him, I asked, "Do you believe me now, Jake? I'm not crazy, I was here."

Jake put up his hands and trying to calm me said, "Yes Caitlyn, I believe you."

That one statement brought the first feelings of peace I had felt in over 2 months and I thanked him for it.

"What are we suppose to do now?" he asked.

"I need to know what happened to Jacob when I left. Did he die April 30, 1883, saving me?" I asked, my emotions showing in my eyes.

"Caitlyn, Jacob lived to be 89 years old, died in 1942 I believe."

This news shocked me at first, then my thoughts turned to the waterfall, getting a strong sense that I needed to go there. "Since Jacob didn't die, I'm sure he would have returned to the cave," I informed him, the feeling getting stronger as I said it. "I need to go to the waterfall, please," I begged.

"Alright, I'll take you there," he told me, "but it'll have to be tomorrow, I have an appointment this afternoon with my Publisher."

Finally putting two and two together I looked at him with astonishment and said, "Oh my God, your J.W. Deppens. I've read some of your books." Understanding dawning now as to why he was so rude at first. He was a friggin celebrity and I was like a crazy stalker.

The half hour Jake had agreed to give me had turned into two hours so I felt it was best for me to leave. I got up, thanking him for his time, and asked, "When should I come tomorrow?"

He told me any time after 9:00 a.m. would be fine and walked me to the door asking, "Are you all right to drive?"

I assured him that the walk to my car would give me enough time to settle down and that I'd be fine. He offered me a ride down, but I refused, not wanting to bother him any further. When I reached the bottom of the porch steps I turned, gave a little wave, and called out, "Thank you so much Jake, I'll see you in the morning."

Caitlyn

The gate was open when I arrived so I turned in the drive. As I got closer I saw the cabin again, and the chills I felt caused goose-bumps to cover my body. After hearing me out Jake had agreed to take me and I was so anxious to go that I didn't sleep at all. Finally I got out of bed around 4:00 a.m. and paced the room for hours. I wasn't sure what I might find up there, if anything, but the feeling to go was strong.

I parked my car and went to the door. Jake answered after my first knock, apparently having heard me arrive. He offered me coffee which I politely refused, since I had already downed a whole pot. I was ready, I couldn't wait any longer. Jake called his dogs, grabbed his rifle, locked up the cabin, and we headed off.

We walked together in silence, his beautiful dogs running ahead, till we reached the path that led through the trees towards the fall. It was a gorgeous Summer day, sunny and warm, but not hot. The path was wide enough for us to walk side-by-side but neither had much to say. My thoughts were racing, my intuition heightened, the need to get there overwhelming.

Approaching the base of the fall Jake spoke for the first time, "This place is beautiful but it always gives me the creeps."

I understood, feelings of trepidation taking over. The last time I was here Jacob and I were being chased by a huge bear and I decided it was best not to share this memory with Jake. I was really glad he had brought his rifle though.

Telling his dogs to stay, we starting up the rock face, Jake at my heels. I pointed, telling him, "There, see that ledge, it leads to a cave."

I don't know if he believed me or not, but he stayed close behind me, steadying me when I slipped a little on the slick rocks. When we reached the ledge I walked behind the curtain of water showing him the rock seat Jacob had told me he used as a boy. Continuing past the seat we entered the cave hidden in the corner.

"I had no idea this was here," Jake told me as he looked around fascinated.

I didn't know what I was suppose to do now that I was here, so I just started looking into all the little crevasses, starting on one side and working my way around. When I got to the corner I reached up and my hand touched something that almost felt like a small animal. I pulled back quickly.

Jake, noting my reaction, came over and said, "Here, let me look." He reached up, felt what I had touched, and pulled it out, handing it to me. It was a rectangular package wrapped in oilcloth and tied with string. Taking the package and hugging it to my chest, I walked to the rock seat and sat down.

As I untied the string, I noticed that Jake was standing back allowing me some privacy. I pulled open the flaps and found a letter, addressed to me in Jacob's handwriting, on top of another wrapped item. My hands started to shake and my heart was beating so fast I was afraid I'd pass out. I took a couple of deep breaths to relax, and opened the seal. Unfolding the yellowed pages, I began to read.

Autumn 1941

My Dearest Caitlyn,

I write to you now an old man, finally, mercifully, near the end of his lonely existence. I'll be making my final visit to the Waterfall today to leave this where I know in my heart, you'll find it.
Sending you away all those years ago was more painful for me than the wounds left by that bear. He tried to kill me Love, I really wish he had, but my dogs wouldn't let him. My Bear was left in pretty bad shape, but Griz made the ultimate sacrifice and gave his life for mine.

Samuel described how he'd found me on the path, mauled up and unconscious. You were nowhere to be found, only a torn scrap of your clothing, leading him to believe that the bear had hauled you away. He sent his sons out to search for you, of course never finding you. I couldn't tell him the truth.

Samuel and his sons carried me to the old cabin and it took Hattie Mae 2 days to get me patched up, and another 2 weeks of tending before I came to. I stayed with them a couple of months, healing, before I could go home.

When I finally went back to the cabin, I didn't want to go in. Entering I walked from room to room, seeing you everywhere, the kitchen, the living room. I stopped in front of the Grandfather Clock, it's pendulum still for the first time in 30 years. I can remember thinking to myself how sad you, and my mother, would have been by this.

I opened the clock's cabinet intent on setting it in motion when a knock on the door interrupted me. Hans was delivering our picture that I had never picked up. He handed me the package and I could feel the frame that I had planned on surprising you with. I paid him and sent him on his way, I'm sure, wondering why I hadn't even looked at it.

I sat on the couch and unwrapped it. God you are beautiful. I cried Caitlyn, really cried for the first time since I was a boy. When I finally stopped I got drunk as hell and made a mess of the place. Instead of starting the clock I wanted to smash it, the only thing stopping me was knowing you never would have forgiven me if I had. I got Isaac and Henry to help me move it to the attic, out of my sight. I never looked at it again.

Emily came for a visit, to check up on me, and after a trip up to see Hattie Mae she came back acting like she had questions to ask, but never did. She tried to convince me to move closer to her but I told her I wouldn't leave. All I had left were my memories of you, and they were strongest in this cabin. I'd NEVER leave it.

I went to the waterfall as soon as I was physically able to climb it and found the cave closed off. I wanted to die Caitlyn, the only thing that kept me from ending it myself was the glimmer of a chance that I might find you again.

The breeder shown up one day with your puppy, the last Griz sired. At first I didn't want him, didn't want to be bothered by a pup, but it didn't take the little guy long to find a small spot in my heart. He looked just like Griz. I named him Copper.

He saved me from myself, gave me a reason to get off my ass and move. He also brought the first smile to my face since you left. Bear took Copper under his wing, I should say paw, and taught him how to behave. I know you would have loved him.

On one of my many trips to the waterfall over the next few years I spotted the bear again giving me a new goal in life, kill the son-of-a-bitch that took you away. I thought killing it would help fill the emptiness in my heart in some way, but it didn't. He weighed almost 700 pounds, and is now a rug that I can stomp on whenever I get the urge.

Well, Caitlyn My Love, I've got to bring this letter to an end so I can make the trip to the cave before nightfall. It takes me a lot longer than it used to, to get there. With this letter I've included our picture, and your I-pod. It stopped working as soon as you were gone.

God Caitlyn, I wish I could hold you one last time. I should have started writing to you years ago. Talking to you with this letter has brought me some small amount of peace.

One last thing I want you to know Love, my soul will find you, just trust your heart.

Yours Eternally,
Jacob

When I finished the letter I looked up and found Jake watching me, my tears flowing freely down my face. I held it out to him and when he took it I unwrapped the second layer of worn leather and looked at the photo. Jacob and I had been so happy, looking at each other instead of the camera with big smiles on our faces, laughing at our shared joke. Anyone seeing this picture would instantly know the love we shared with each other.

Fresh tears spilled from my eyes as my thoughts returned to Jacob's words. He had written the letter a few months before his death, at the age of 89. My God, 59 years he had lived, all alone. I opened the last little item and found my I-pod, the metal case rusty. It was, after all, 130 years old.

With my mind lost in thought, I was startled with Jake's words, "May I see the picture?" Handing it to him I watched to see his reaction. Staring at the picture, shaking his head slightly, then looking back at me he said, "You really were there. How does something like this happen?"

I didn't know what to say to his question so I just shook my head, "I can't explain any of this . . . Jacob and I tried to figure out why in the beginning, then we just decided it was a gift from God, and enjoyed each other. I'll probably never know."

"The bear rug he mentioned in the letter is rolled up in the attic. I always hated it," Jake said, finishing with, "I think I'll pull it out of there and have it destroyed."

Jake could tell that I was emotionally wasted and offered his hand to help me up, "Come on Caitlyn, let me get you back to the cabin."

I was ready to leave, I had found what I was looking for, the validation that Jacob and I had been together, it hadn't been just a dream.

On the walk back I realized that I couldn't tell anyone about this. I would never be able to share this with my family. Jake would be the only person who knew the whole story and I wanted it to stay that way.

I stopped abruptly and turned to him, "Please promise me you'll never tell anyone about all this, I can't stand the thought of sharing this with the world."

"It'll be our secret," he assured me.

I don't know why but I knew I could trust him.

Walking in the door of the cabin, the Grandfather clock bonging one, Jake asked, "Can I get you anything? Are you hungry?"

I wasn't hungry but said nothing, so he went on, "I could fix you some eggs. It's about the only thing I know how to cook properly."

His words stirred the memory of Jacob in my heart, renewing the searing pain of his loss, and I knew I had to get out of there. I needed to be alone for awhile. Thanking him for his help, I told him I had to go, and almost running I went to my car, got in, and drove away.

Jake

After Caitlyn left the cabin a few days ago, I sat for hours, my mind going over, and over, the events of the previous two days. The whole thing was so totally unbelievable, but there was definite proof that she had been here all those years ago. The woman in the sepia picture was Caitlyn, her beautiful face had been alight with laughter. I wanted to see her like that, happy and laughing. Hell, I just wanted to see her again.

I had no idea where she was staying, or if she was even still in town. I never should have let her leave, as upset as she was, and I needed to know she was alright. Picking up the phone, and punching in the number for information, I got the phone numbers for some of the local hotels in the area. Starting with the first one, I called and ask the desk clerk if there was a Caitlyn Jacobs registered there. By the sixth, Sorry Sir, I slammed down the phone, totally frustrated, and got up, walking out the back door to the porch.

Standing there, leaning against the railing, my thoughts on the woman I met just a week ago. How was I ever going to find her? Jacobs was a common name and I had no idea which state to even begin looking in. I didn't want to ask anyone to help me because word could leak out that I was looking for some mystery woman, and if the tabloids got wind of it, I could just see the headlines, "Jake Deppens searches for his Cinderella."

Not knowing what else to do, I headed to the barn, hoping that a workout would help clear my mind. The dogs trailing me as far as the barn before taking off on their latest adventure. Pulling off my shirt, I laid on the bench and started with some presses. After about an hour of pushing my body to it's limit, Caitlyn was still in my head. I had to find her, some how, some way, I had to.

Why she was such an obsession, I didn't know. Walking to the barn door I leaned against the frame, hoping to take a little pleasure in the light Summer breeze to help cool off my overheated body. While looking towards the cabin, an image flooded my mind, Caitlyn on horseback, riding away from me, her coppery hair flying out behind her, then another of her holding a shovel, giving me a contemptuous look. Her sexy body in jeans and a tight red shirt.

The inspiration for a new spitfire character inhabited my brain and I headed quickly back to the cabin, and my laptop. I put on a pot of coffee, knowing it was going to be a long night, and ran up for a quick shower. When I got back downstairs, I poured myself a big mug full and sat.

As soon as my fingers touched the keyboard the words started flowing, using Caitlyn as my muse. For the next 16 hours I typed steady, taking only necessary breaks for nature's calls, and to stretch while refilling my cup. I had never enjoyed one of my characters as much as I did Kat.

Finishing the final chapters and putting them in a file, I hit the send button, addressed to my Publisher, knowing she'd be as pleased with the outcome as I was. Exhausted I headed up to bed and fell asleep immediately, sweet dreams of Caitlyn giving me the best night's sleep I'd ever had.

For the next six months I spent my time reading Kathryn's Journals, which, like Caitlyn had said, were some of the best books I'd ever read. My three-times Great Grandmother was so adept at capturing her thoughts and emotions in her words, that she was able to bring her experience to life for the reader. I prayed I was half as good a writer as she had been.

I also devoted a lot of my time to working on my next book, my new character, Kat, front and center. When my last novel had been released in October, featuring her, it shot to the top of the best seller's list, and still occupied the number one slot. My readers loved her as much as I did. The images of Caitlyn that flooded my mind constantly were my true inspiration. When I had named her Kat I hadn't realized it was Kathryn's nickname but I think from what I know about her from reading her journals, she would have been pleased. The two women had a lot in common.

I heard the Grandfather clock, it's chimes announcing the upcoming hour. I hadn't known it's history before Caitlyn, that it had been a gift to Kathryn from her husband on the day his son was born. My mother had found the clock wrapped in the attic and it wouldn't start. My father had it fixed as a surprise to her on the day I was born. It was funny how history had repeated itself.

I returned the journals to their hiding place for safe keeping and when I opened the panel I noticed another small package that I had missed when I took them out. Unwrapping it I found two hair combs in the shape of butterfly wings. Holding them together I got a strong image of Caitlyn, completely naked, turning slowly. When I saw the back of her head the two combs were on each side of her long braid forming the butterfly.

This image of Caitlyn wasn't a fantasy, it was a memory. She was so alluring that my body responded in a way it never had before. I wanted her more than I'd ever wanted any woman. Sitting back with that thought in my head, I realized I was in love with Caitlyn. She had opened up something in my heart that only she would be able to fill.

My need to find Caitlyn intensified. Over the months I have tried to find her, searching each state's records, one by one. I was surprised with how many Caitlyn Jacobs' there were in the U.S. Not having anything to go on, not even a birth date, only her name, made the search difficult, but I was determined to find her. Somehow, someway, I'd find her.

Florida popped into my head. I hadn't gotten to the southern states yet but right after Christmas I was going to start in Florida. That's where she was, I was sure of it.

Caitlyn

Leaving the cabin after our trip to the waterfall, I drove back to my hotel room, and stayed there, crying for two straight days. Thoughts of Jacob and his lonely life, holding me in the grips of despair. The six months I had with him were real, and I exulted in their memory, cherishing every single moment.

I stayed in town for the rest of the week, my mind drifting to Jake quite often. He had believed in me, and helped me more than anyone else could have. He was a good man, a bit grumpy at times, but I owed him a dept of gratitude. Not wanting to intrude on his life any further I decided it was time for me to go home.

Packing up my car, I got in and drove through town, stopping on the side of the road to look at the mountains one last time. Standing there, my tears streaming down my face, I knew I had to let Jacob go. After a whispered, "Good bye My Love," I got back in my car and headed south, in the direction of my Grandparent's house. It was time for me to get back to my life, and after a couple of weeks with them, and a teary goodbye, I flew home to Florida.

For the next few months my life resumed some sense of normality. Wynie and I talked every day, enjoying the love and friendship we shared. My whole family flew up together to my Grandparent's home for Thanksgiving, making up for the trip we missed. It was wonderful, the only thing bittersweet was my solitary walk in my secret garden.

I couldn't feel Jacob's presence anymore, he was gone from my life now. My spirit had gone on a journey to meet his, but now the journey was over and all I had were the memories of the soul. Saying one last tearful goodbye, I headed back to the house, to my family who loved me.

As the months passed, the pain of losing Jacob eased slightly and my thoughts frequently turned to Jake. In a way my search for Jacob had led me to him. Believing that everything happened for a reason, I felt that one day our paths would cross again.

Before I knew it, Christmas was here. Wynie and I drove up to our parent's home in Palm Beach to spend a few festive days with them. On Christmas morning me and Wynie were like little kids, tearing our presents open with zeal. When I opened one from her I was pleasantly surprised with the latest J.W. Deppen's novel.

Turning it over I stared at the picture of Jake's handsome face, sans the beard, on the book cover. The slight smirk on his face showing off his dimples to their greatest advantage and caused a stirring sensation to move through me. Hearing my sister say, "God, he's a hunk," brought me out of my reverie, and I smiled at her, agreeing, and thanked her for her gift.

After a wonderful Christmas day with my family, I said Goodnight to all and headed up to my old bedroom, carrying Jake's book in my hand. After a little bedtime prep, I jumped into bed, sitting up, and opened the book to the dedication. As I read his words my heart soared.

This book is dedicated to a very special lady, you know who you are. Without you, I never would have finished it. You evoked the memories of my soul. Sooner, or later, I'll find you.

His declaration caused a yearning in me, sending a sort of shockwave through my being. Knowing that his words had probably caused a hailstorm in Celebrity-ville, brought a smile to my face. He liked his privacy and I'm sure this dedication had the paparazzi swarming. I felt pleasure knowing he was searching for me, and just maybe, it was time for him to find me.

Over the next two days I devoured his book, his new character, Kat, seemed so familiar, especially when she told Colton Slade that he was rude, and lacking in manners. One scene was so reminiscent of something Jacob and I had shared that it brought tears to my eyes.

Closing the book when I was finished, I started making plans. Two more days with my parents and sister, and I headed for my home.

Checking the weather in the area of Ellenburg I found that my trip there was possible. I picked up the phone and made all the arrangements. Letting my sister know that I was going out of town for a while, without giving all the details, proved to be a little tricky. She could be really nosey some times, but I loved her for that too. The next morning the cab picked me up, and then dropped me off 20 minutes later at the airport.

The flight was uneventful, my anxiety revving. Jumping into my rental car, map in hand, I headed in the direction of Ellenburg Township and Laclair Road. Reaching my destination, I pulled off the road in front of his property, and noticed he still had the same signs, posting, "No Trespassing," and now "Bad Dogs." Laughing to myself I headed to the weak spot in his fence, squeezing through, just like the last time.

About half way up to the cabin I was boisterously welcomed by Onyx and Copper, their loud barking, I'm sure alerting Jake to my presence. I was vigorously petting and playing with them when he came into view. He looked like an oversized woodsman in his heavy coat, rifle in hand. I stood up to my full height, possibly reaching his chin, as he came towards me. When he was a couple of feet in front of me, he stopped, giving me that roguish look of his.

"Mr. Deppens, so nice to see you again," I greeted, my emotions evident in my tear filled eyes.

"Oh, it's you, the pest," he answered, his smile widening as his eyes showed pleasure.

We just stood there devouring each other with our eyes, the chills running through my body having nothing to do with the wintry temperature.

After a few minutes of just taking each other in, Jake dropped his rifle and opened his arms in welcome, saying, "Come home Caitlyn."

I walked into his longed-for embrace with a sense of joy I never thought I'd feel again, trusting in my heart and soul, that I was, truly home.

Epilogue
April, 2013

The following Spring Jake and Caitlyn were married in a private ceremony held near the base of the waterfall, surrounded by the beauty of the season. The only witnesses to this blissful union, their immediate families and close personal friends.

The bride wore a floor-length ivory gown, modest in fashion that draped her body in feminine elegance. Her waist length copper hair was styled in a loose French braid that cascaded over her left shoulder, and was adorned with two sapphire and diamond hair combs that formed a butterfly, heirlooms that had been in the groom's family for over 100 years. The deep blue of the sapphires emphasizing the bride's sparkling eyes.

The groom was casually attired in denim jeans, and a royal blue dress shirt that accentuated his smiling blue eyes, which he couldn't seem to keep off his new wife. The tenderness he showed when he picked his bride up in his arms and finished their first dance brought tears to the eyes of all their guests.

The couple enjoy a reclusive lifestyle, avoiding the limelight, and the hoards of paparazzi eager to get the first picture of the newlyweds together. For months they tried to get a picture of J.W. Deppens and his wife, the elusive Caitlyn. When one photographer was finally lucky enough to catch them, you could see the happiness in their faces as they gazed into each other's eyes, laughing with pure joy, on the front of every magazine. The words, "Match Made In Heaven," the headlines.

Here's What's Cookin Golden Raisin Buns
From the Kitchen of: Barbara Yates

Ingredients: **Buns**

1 cup Water
½ cup Butter
1 teaspoon Sugar
¼ teaspoon Salt
1 cup all purpose Flour
4 Eggs
½ cup Golden Raisins, plumped in boiling water and drained thoroughly

Lemon Frosting

1 Tablespoon Butter
1 ½ Tablespoon Heavy Cream
1 cup Confectioner's Sugar
½ teaspoon fresh Lemon Juice
½ teaspoon Vanilla Extract

Directions: Combine water, butter, sugar and salt in a medium saucepan and bring to a boil. Turn down burner to low heat and add flour all at once and beat with a wooden spoon about 1 minute or until mixture leaves sides of pan and forms a smooth thick dough. Remove from heat and continue beating about 2 minutes to cool slightly. Add eggs one at a time beating after each addition until mixture has a satin sheen. (This is an excellent workout for the arms and is definitely worth the effort put in.) Stir in Raisins. Drop heaping tablespoons about 2 inches apart on a greased baking sheet. Bake in preheated 375 degree oven for 30 to 35 minutes or until doubled in size, golden and firm. Remove to a wire rack to cool slightly. To make the frosting: In medium saucepan melt 1 tablespoon of butter; stir in 1 ½ tablespoons of heavy cream. Remove from heat and stir in 1 cup confectioner's sugar until smooth. Stir in ½ tsp. fresh lemon juice and ½ tsp. vanilla. While still warm, gently spread frosting over tops and sides. Makes 14-16 of the most delicious Buns you've ever sunk your teeth into. Just ask Jacob!

Book Reviews

Heather Kaplan
Hi aunt Barb! Started *Memories of the Soul* yesterday afternoon and just finished. You are sooo amazingly talented!!! Brought tears to my eyes. I'm anxiously awaiting the second one. Call me if you want and we can talk more. Love you <3
****

Alina Lawrence
Hi Barbara, I am sorry it has taken me so long to get back to you but here is my review. I have to say I was a little nervous to read it at first, I thought to myself 'what if I don't like it, how could I tell her something negative?' but that was definitely NOT a problem, because I loved it from the very beginning! This was really an enjoyable read and I look forward to reading many more even if I have to wait for them to be published. The whole idea was so original and well thought out. Everything just read so smoothly and connected together seamlessly. I wish I had the book here so I could go back through and pin point exact paragraphs and instances . . . actually, I would love to read it again and write this as I read but off the top of my head . . . . I loved the way the point of view went back and forth between the characters, seeing some of the same events as they were seen and felt from each person's perspective. Throughout the book I was able to feel the emotions of the characters . . . I laughed out loud; I even cried and had goose bumps!

Caitlyn was feisty, yet lady like . . . . she was feminine but strong. She was beautiful and funny, everyone loved her, and she was a perfect housewife too! She loved her man and his family, had good friends, she had talents and hobbies. She had her own interests as well as hopes and dreams. I enjoyed there was a little of you in her too like the cooking and photography. I am definitely going to be making those pancakes in the near future because they sound yummy! She was happy in the moment and was satisfied with almost nothing just to have love and happiness in her life . . . what I think are the most important things to have . . . and after some tribulations and determination she was rewarded with all that and more. She got love and beauty, she got her man, she got her family, and even some fame.

Jacob was handsome, strong, kind, sexy, he was a good provider and protector. He was a hard worker and he wanted to give her the world. He enjoyed that she cooked and took care of him but he also appreciated that she was her own person as well and supported the things she wanted to do.

Your descriptions of the scenery and places and events were so vivid I could just see them all in my mind and I loved the setting . . . a cabin in the mountains, the seasons changing, especially when the sun was rising through the V of the mountains and the sun was lighting up the clouds from beneath. I could totally see that image in my mind's eye and it was beautiful, I wanted to be there.

I was sad that it ended. But it was perfect for someone like me that likes to be able to read a good book in a few nights, cause I don't have a lot of time during the day with the baby and the house, but it would also be perfect for people who like to stretch their books out and read a little here and a little there. You should be so proud of yourself and you should pursue this till the end. Not everyone has the courage, drive, or even the talent to pursue their dreams and you have them all! So go for it! I really enjoyed this so much and hope to be able to read more in the future.
****
Debbie Baum
I finished the book!!! And I LOVED it!! When I finally got to sit down and read last night I couldn't put it down. I read and read and read . . . I had to put eye drops in my eyes . . . lol. I really did love it and I wouldn't change a thing. I liked how it was her story and then his story, not just one person doing all the story telling. and like I said it was a mystery and a love story. I was both happy and sad at the end. It was wonderful. REALLY! I mean it. Get started on that sequel . . . lol. You might just make me a reader again. Happy Thanksgiving to you all!!!
****

Roberta Domblewski

Dear Barbara, I enjoyed reading your book. I enjoyed having Jacob and Caitlyn tell their side of the story. I especially liked the ending which was a surprise to me. Your creative twist to the whole story was refreshing. I found your chapters very easy reading and did not become confused with characters. Speaking of characters, I wished that you would have told me more about the lives of Samuel and Hattie Mae (especially their escape from slavery.) I was also fascinated by Louisa (Jacob's lover.) I enjoyed Kathryn's Journals and would have loved to have read more about her life.

I am glad that Bernie shared your book with me. I wish you much success. Keep writing. If you are ever up this way, we could have a book signing at our Book Station. I loved your dogs too! Thanks for sharing

****

Edith House

I read you story with much delight. Having lost my husband (love of my life) 10 years ago I had that same feeling Caitlyn did when she woke with such want. I often, in the first years, dreamed about my husband and didn't want to wake.

Your characters seem to leap off the page and settle into the deepest part of ones heart who once loved truly.

Beautifully written and a beautiful ending—leaving the reader with the hope of being together once again.

****

Katelyn

I thought the book was absolutely amazing. I wouldn't change a thing. I would love to read more so hopefully you'll write some more.